Pericles on 31st Street

by Harry Mark Petrakis

LION AT MY HEART

THE ODYSSEY OF KOSTAS VOLAKIS

PERICLES ON 31ST STREET

Pericles on 31st Street

HARRY MARK PETRAKIS

Chicago | *Quadrangle Books* | 1965

"Pericles on 31st Street (under the title, "Pericles on 34th Street"), "Courtship of the Blue Widow," "Pa and the Sad Turkeys," "The Legacy of Leontis," and "The Passing of the Ice" orginally appeared in the *Atlantic;* "The Ballad of Daphne and Apollo" (under the title, "A Knowledge of Her Past"), "A Hand for Tomorrow" (under the title, "The Little Store on Bleecker Street"), and "The Wooing of Ariadne" in the *Saturday Evening Post;* "The Miracle" in *Playboy;* "The Return of Katerina" in *Greek Heritage;* "The Eyes of Love" in *Cavalier,* "Matsoukas" in *Chicago Magazine;* "The Song of Rhodanthe" in *Country Beautiful;* "The Prison" in *Chicago Review;* and "The Journal of a Wife-Beater" in *Harper's Bazaar.*

Third Printing

For My Sons,

MARK, JOHN, AND DEAN

PERICLES ON 31st STREET

Louie Debella's bar was located on the corner of 31st Street and Dart Avenue, the last store in a group of five stores owned by Leonard Barsevick, who besides being a landlord operated the Lark Wholesale Clothing Company across the street.

My name is George. My last name is not important. I'm Louie Debella's night bartender and I count myself a good bartender. I might mention a few of the quality places I have tended bar, but that has nothing to do with this story.

If I have learned anything from fifteen years of tending bar it is that a bartender cannot take sides with anything that goes on across the bar. He has got to be strictly non-partisan. A cousin of mine in South Bend, also in the business, once tried to mediate an argument about Calvin Coolidge. Somebody hit him in the back of the head with a bottle of beer that was not yet empty, and besides needing stitches he got wet. Now when I am on the job I never take sides. That is, I never did until the episode of Pericles.

As I understand it this fellow Pericles was a Greek general and statesman who lived back in those Greek golden years you read about in the school history books. From all reports he was a pretty complete sort of guy who laid down a set of rules and was tough on everybody who did not read them right.

If you are wondering what a Greek who lived a couple of thousand years ago has got to do with this story, I guess it all started because the storekeepers in our row of stores gathered in the bar in the evening after they locked their doors for a glass of beer.

The first man in was usually Dan Ryan, who had the butcher shop. Ryan was a heavy beer man and needed the head start on the others. A little later Olaf Johnson, who ran the Sunlight lunchroom, came in with Sol Reidman the tailor. Olaf had a huge belly that was impossible to keep under a coat. Sol liked nothing better than to tease Olaf about when the triplets were expected.

The last man in was Bernard Klioris, who had a little grocery next to Sol's tailor shop. Bernard usually got lost in the arguments, and swung back and forth like a kitchen door in a restaurant. He had a sad thin face and was not so bright, but among our patrons you could hardly tell.

Last Tuesday night after I had served Ryan his fourth beer, Olaf and Sol and Bernard came in together, with Olaf and Sol arguing as usual.

"She told me she was a Republican," Olaf said. "They want some lunk for Congress. I told her to come by you and get her petition signed."

Sol waggled his bald head indignantly. "Who gave you leave to advertise my business?" he said. "A man's politics is a sacred trust that belongs to him alone."

"She only had a petition, not a gun," Olaf said. "I knew you was a Republican so I sent her."

"How can anyone," Ryan said from the bar, "be in his right mind and still be a Republican?"

Sol waved a warning finger. "Be careful," he said. "You are stepping on the Constitution when you ridicule a man's politics."

"I read about the Constitution," Bernard said.

They lined up at the bar. I poured them beer. All they ever drank was beer.

The door opened and Nick Simonakis came in. He was the vendor who took his stand at night on the corner of 31st and Dart. He had a glassed-in wagon that he pushed into place under the street lamp, and from the wagon he sold hot dogs and tamales and peanuts. Several times during the evening he locked up the wagon and came into the bar for a glass of wine. He would sit alone at a table to the side of the room, his dark eyes in his hollow-checked face glaring at the room from above the white handlebar mustache. Every now and then he would sip his wine and shake his head, making his thick white hair hang more disordered over his forehead.

Other men might have thought he was a little crazy because sometimes he sat there alone talking to himself, but like I said, I do not take sides. At other times he gave up muttering and loudly berated the drinkers of beer. "Only Turks would drink beer," he said, "when they could drink wine. One for the belly and the other for wisdom." He would sip his wine slowly, mocking their guzzling of beer, and the storekeepers would try to ignore him.

"The sun-ripened grapes," Simonakis said, "hanging until they become sweet. Then the trampling by the young maidens to extract the lovely juices. A ceremony of the earth."

"Beer don't just grow in barrels," Olaf said. "Good beer takes a lot of making."

The old man laughed softly as if he was amused. "You are a Turk," he said. "I excuse you because you think and talk like a Turk."

"Say, old man," Sol said. "Someone wants a bag of peanuts. You are losing business."

Simonakis looked at Sol with bright piercing eyes. "I will lose business," he said. "I am drinking my wine."

"He must be rich," Ryan said, "and pushing business away. I wish I had gone into peddling peanuts myself."

"It is not a case of wealth," Simonakis said. "There is a time for labor and a time for leisure. A man must have time to sit and think. This made Greece great."

"Made who what?" Olaf asked with sarcasm.

The old man swept him with contempt. "In ancient Greece," he said coldly, "an elephant like you would have been packed on a mountaintop as bait for buzzards."

"Watch the language," Olaf said. "I don't have to take that stuff from an old goat like you."

"A land of ruined temples," Sol said, and he moved from the bar and carried his beer to a nearby table. "A land of philosophers without shoes."

"A land of men!" Simonakis spit out. "We gave the world learning and courage. We taught men how to live and how to die."

Ryan and Bernard and Olaf had followed Sol to the table, drawing their chairs.

"Would you mind, old man," Ryan said as he sat down, "leaving a little bit of credit to the Irish?"

"I give them credit," Simonakis said, "for inventing the wheelbarrow, and giving the world men to push it."

"Did you hear that!" Ryan said indignantly and looked fiercely at the old man.

The old man went on as if he had not heard. "A model

of courage for the world," he said. "Leonidas with three hundred men holding the pass at Thermopylae against the Persian hordes. Themistocles destroying the great fleet of Xerxes at Salamis."

"That's history," Olaf said. "What have they done lately?"

Simonakis ignored him. He motioned to me and I took him the bottle of port. He raised the full glass and held it up and spoke in Greek to the wine as if performing some kind of ceremony. The men watched him and somebody laughed. Simonakis glared at them. "Laugh, barbarians," he said. "Laugh and forget your debt to Greece. Forget the golden age and the men like lions. Hide in your smoking cities and drown in your stinking beer."

"What a goat," Olaf said.

Sol shook his head sadly. "It is a pity to see a man ruined by drink," he said. "That wine he waves has soaked his head."

"Wheelbarrow indeed," Ryan said, and he glared back at the old man.

2

AT THAT MOMENT the front door opened and Leonard Barsevick, the landlord, walked in. He carried an air of elegance into the bar. Maybe because of his Homburg and the black chesterfield coat he wore.

The storekeepers greeted him in a respectful chorus. He waved his hand around like a politician at a beer rally and smiled broadly. "Evening, boys," he said. "Only got a minute but I couldn't pass by without stopping to buy a few of my tenants a beer. George, set up the drinks and mark it on my tab."

"Thank you, Mr. Barsevick," Olaf said. "You sure look like a million bucks tonight."

Barsevick laughed and looked pleased. "Got to keep up

a front, Olaf," he said. "If a man in my position gets a spot on his suit he might as well give up."

"That's right, Mr. Barsevick," Ryan said. "A man in your position has got to keep up with the best and you sure do."

"Say, Mr. Barsevick," Bernard said. "You know the leak in the roof at my store I spoke to you about last month. It hasn't been fixed yet and that rain the other night . . ."

"Wait a minute, Bernie," Barsevick laughed. "Not tonight. If I promised to fix it, I'm going to have it fixed. Leonard Barsevick is a man of his word. Ain't that right, boys?"

They all nodded and Olaf said, "Yes, sir," emphatically.

"But not tonight," Barsevick said. "Tonight I'm out for a little relaxation with a baby doll that looks like Jayne Mansfield." He made a suggestive noise with his mouth.

"You're sure a lucky man, Mr. Barsevick," Olaf said admiringly.

"Not luck at all, Olaf," Barsevick said, and his voice took on a tone of serious confidence. "It's perseverance and the ability to get along with people. I always say if I didn't know how to get along with people I wouldn't be where I am today."

"That's sure right, Mr. Barsevick," Ryan said. The others nodded agreement.

"Fine," Barsevick beamed. "All right, boys, drink up, and pass your best wishes to Leonard Barsevick for a successful evening." He winked broadly.

The storekeepers laughed and raised their glasses. Everybody toasted Barsevick but Simonakis. He sat scowling at the landlord from beneath his shaggy brows. Barsevick noticed him.

"You didn't give this gentleman a drink, George," he said. "What are you drinking, sir?"

"He ain't no gentleman," Olaf said. "He is a peanut peddler."

"An authority on wheelbarrows," Ryan said.

Simonakis cocked a thumb at Barsevick. "Hurry, landlord," he said, "your Mansfield is waiting."

Barsevick gave him a cool glance, but the old man just looked bored. Finally the landlord gave up and turned away, pulling on his suede gloves. He strode to the door cutting a fancy figure and waved grandly. "Good night, boys," he said.

The boys wished him good night. Simonakis belched.

3

On the following Thursday the notices came from Barsevick's bookkeeper announcing a fifteen per cent rent increase all along the block. All the storekeepers got a notice of the raise becoming effective with the expiration of their leases about a month away. Louie was so disturbed he called me down in the middle of the afternoon and took off early.

That night the storekeepers were a sad bunch. They sat around the table over their beer, looking like their visas had expired.

"I don't understand it," Ryan said. "Mr. Barsevick knows that business has not been good. Fifteen per cent at this time makes for an awful load."

"With license fees and the rest," Olaf said, "a lunchroom ain't hardly worth while. I was not making nothing before. With this increase it ain't going to get no better."

"Two hands to sew pants will not be enough," Sol said. "I must sew with four hands, all my own."

Bernard looked distressed. "Mr. Barsevick must have a good reason," he said.

"He's got expenses," Olaf said.

"He should have mine," Ryan said. "Beef is up six cents a pound again."

Simonakis came into the bar pulling off his gloves. He ignored the men as he walked by them to his table against the wall and signaled to me for his bottle of wine.

"I am going to buy a wagon," Olaf said loudly, "and sell peanuts and hot dogs on the street."

"You must first," Simonakis said, "have the wisdom to tell them apart."

Olaf flushed and started to get up. Sol shook him down. "No time for games with crazy men tonight," Sol said. "This matter is serious. We must organize a delegation to speak to Mr. Barsevick. It must be explained that this increase imposes a terrible burden on us at this time. Perhaps a little later."

"Shoot him," Simonakis said. He waved the glass I had just filled with dark wine.

"You mind your own business, peddler," Ryan said. "Nobody is talking to you."

"A Greek would shoot him," Simonakis said. "But you are toads."

"I get my rent raised," Olaf said, "and now I got to sit here and be insulted by a peanut peddler."

The front door opened and the room went quiet.

Barsevick closed the door softly behind him and walked over to the storekeepers' table and pulled up a chair and sat down like a sympathetic friend coming to share their grief.

I guess they were all as surprised as I was and for a long moment no one spoke and Barsevick looked solemnly from one to the other. "I hope you do not mind my butting in, boys," he said and he motioned to me. "George, bring the boys a round on me."

"Mr. Barsevick," Ryan said, "the boys and me were just discussing . . ."

Barsevick raised his hand gravely. "I know, Danny," he said. "I know what you are going to say. I want to go on record first as saying there is nobody any sorrier than Leonard Barsevick about this. That is why I am here. My bookkeeper said I did not have to come over tonight and talk to you. I told him I would not stand for that, that you boys were not just tenants, you were friends of mine."

"It is a lot of money, Mr. Barsevick," Olaf said. "I mean if we were making more, things might be different."

"I know that, Olaf," Barsevick said. "Believe me, if there was any other way I would jump at the chance. I said to Jack, my bookkeeper, 'Isn't there any other way?' I swear to you boys he said, 'Mr. Barsevick, if that rent is not increased it will be charity.' " I brought the tray of fresh beer and set the glasses around the table. "Not that I mind a little help to my friends," Barsevick said, "but it is not good business. I would be shamed before my competitors. 'There's Barsevick,' they would laugh, 'too soft to raise his tenants' rent.' They would put the screws on me and in no time at all I might be out of business."

Everybody was silent for a moment, probably examining the prospect of Leonard Barsevick put out of business because of his soft heart.

"We know you got expenses," Ryan said.

Barsevick shook his head mournfully. "You got no idea," he said. "I mean you boys got no idea. I am afraid sometimes for the whole economy. Costs cannot keep rising and still keep the country sound. Everything is going up. Believe me, boys, being a landlord and a businessman is hell."

"Shoot him," Simonakis said loudly.

Barsevick stopped talking and looked across the tables at the old man.

"He is a crazy man," Sol said. "That wine he drinks makes him talk to himself."

Barsevick turned back to the men but he was disturbed. He looked over at the old man once more like he was trying to understand and then started to get up. "I got to go now, boys," he said. "I'm working late tonight with my bookkeeper. If we see any other way to cut costs I will be glad to reconsider the matter of the increase. That is my promise to you boys as friends."

"We sure appreciate you stopping by, Mr. Barsevick," Ryan said. "We know there is many a landlord would not have bothered."

Barsevick shook his head vigorously. "Not Leonard Barsevick," he said. "Not even his worst enemy will say that Barsevick does not cut a straight corner when it comes to friends."

"We know that, Mr. Barsevick," Olaf said.

"We sure do," Bernard said.

"Shoot him," Simonakis said. "Shoot him before he gets away."

4

BARSEVICK whirled around and stared in some kind of shock at the old man. I guess he was trying very fast to figure out if the old man was serious.

"Don't pay him no mind, Mr. Barsevick," Olaf said. "He has been out in the rain too long."

"You are a demagogue." Simonakis spoke loudly to the landlord. "You wave your greedy fingers and tell them you are a friend. Aaaaaaaaa!" The old man smiled craftily. "I know your kind. In Athens they would tie you under a bull."

Barsevick stood there like rocks were being bounced off his head, his face turning a bright shade of red.

Sol motioned angrily at the old man. "Somebody wants a hot dog," he said. "You are losing business."

Simonakis looked at Sol for a moment with his mustache bristling, then looked at the others. "I have lost business," he said slowly. "You have lost courage."

A sound of hissing came from Barsevick, his red cheeks shaking off heat like a capped kettle trying to let off steam. "You goddam pig," he said huskily. "You unwashed old bum. You damn peddler of peanuts."

The old man would not give an inch. "You are a hypocrite," he said. "A hypocrite and a libertine. You live on the sweat of better men."

Barsevick's jaw was working furiously like he was trying to chew up the right words.

"Let me tell you," Simonakis said, and his voice took on a more moderate tone as if he were pleased to be able to pass information on to the landlord, "let me tell you how the hypocrite goes in the end. One day the people wake up. They know he is a liar and a thief. They pick up stones. They aim for his head." He pointed a big long finger at Barsevick and made a rattling sound rise from his throat. "What a mess a big head like yours would make."

Barsevick gasped and whirled to the men at the table. "He's threatening me," he shouted. "Did you hear him? Throw the old bastard out."

No one moved. I kept wiping glasses. A good bartender learns to keep working.

"Did you hear me!" Barsevick yelled. "Somebody throw him out."

"He is a crazy old man," Sol said. "He talks without meaning."

"Shut up!" Barsevick said. "You stick with him because you are no damn good either."

"I do not stick with him," Sol said, and he drew himself up hurt. "I am trying to be fair."

Barsevick turned to me. "George, throw him out!"

I kept wiping the glasses. "I am underpaid, Mr. Barsevick," I said. "My salary barely covers my work. Any extra service would be charity."

The old man took after him again. "Who likes you, landlord?" he said. "Be honest and speak truth before your tenants. Who likes you?"

"You shut up!" Barsevick shouted.

"I mean really likes you," Simonakis said. "I do not mean the poor girls you buy with your tainted money."

"I'll shut the old bastard up!" Barsevick hollered and started for the table against the wall.

Simonakis stood up and Barsevick stopped. The old man looked tall and menacing with his big hands and bright eyes and his white mustache standing out like a joyous challenge to battle. "You cannot shut up truth," Simonakis said. "And the truth is that you are a leech feeding on the labor of better men. You wish to become rich by making them poorer."

Barsevick stood a couple of tables away from the old man with his back bent a little waiting for a word to be raised in his defense. No one spoke and the old man stared at him with eyes like knives.

"You old bastard . . . " Barsevick said weakly.

Ryan made a sound clearing his throat. He wore a stern and studied look on his face. "Fifteen per cent is a steep raise," he said. "Right at this time when it is tough to make ends meet."

Barsevick whirled on him. "You keep out of this," he said. "You just mind your own business."

"I would say," Ryan said slowly, "fifteen per cent more rent to pay each month is my business."

"I'll make it twenty-five per cent," Barsevick shouted. "If you don't like it you can get out!"

"I have a lease," Ryan said quietly. He was looking at the landlord like he was seeing him for the first time.

"I will break it," Barsevick said. He looked angrily around at the other storekeepers. "I will break all your leases."

"I did not say nothing!" Bernard protested.

"The way of tyrants and thieves," Simonakis said. "All who oppose them suffer." He raised his head and fixed his eyes upon the ceiling. "O Pericles, lend us a stick so we may drive the tyrant from the market place."

"Stop calling me a tyrant," Barsevick fumed.

Simonakis kept his head raised praying to that guy Pericles.

"I'm going to put every one of you into the street," Barsevick said. "I'm going to teach you all not to be so damn smart."

Sol shook his head with measured contempt for the landlord on his face. "You will not put us out," he said. "First, you are too greedy for the rent. Second, you would not rent those leaking barns again without major repairs, and third . . ." He paused. "Third, I do not admire your personality."

"Amen," Bernard said. "My roof keeps leaking."

"O Pericles!" Simonakis suddenly cried out and everybody looked at him. "They are barbarians and not of Athens but they are honest men and need your help. Give them strength to destroy the common enemy. Lend them your courage to sweep out the tyrant."

"You are all crazy," Barsevick said and he looked driven and disordered. His tie was outside his coat and the Homburg perched lopsided over one ear.

"You are a tiger," Sol said. "Tell me what circus you live in and I will rent a cage to take you home."

"Do not be insulting," Ryan said to Sol. "You will hurt

the landlord's feelings. He cannot help he has got a head like a loin of pork."

"You ignorant bastards!" Barsevick shouted.

Ryan got up and came over to the bar. He stepped behind and pulled out the little sawed-off bat Louie kept under the counter. He winked at me. "I am just borrowing it," he said. "I want to put a new crease in the landlord's hat."

Simonakis came back from calling on Pericles. "Do not strike him," he said. "Stone him. Stone him as they stoned tyrants in Athens." He looked at the floor and around the room excitedly searching for stones.

Barsevick in full retreat began to edge toward the door. He opened his mouth to try and speak some final word of defiance but one look at the bat in Ryan's hands must have choked off his wind.

"Tyrant!" Simonakis shouted.

"Vulture!" Olaf said. "Stop and eat on me, and I'll grind some glass for your salad!"

"Greedy pig!" Ryan said, and he waved the bat. "You try and collect that rent and we all move out!"

"Judas!" Sol said. "Come to me only to sew your shroud!"

"Fix my leaking roof!" Bernard said.

With one last helpless wail, Barsevick stumbled out through the door.

For a long moment after the door closed nobody moved. Then Ryan handed me back the bat. I put it under the counter. Olaf started to the bar with his glass. Bernard came after him. Soon all were lined up at the bar. All except Simonakis, who had gone back to sit down at his table staring moodily into his glass of wine.

Ryan turned his back to the bar and looked across the tables at Simonakis. He looked at him for a long time and no one spoke. The old man kept staring at his wine. Ryan looked back helplessly at Olaf and Sol and they watched him struggling. Bernard looked dazed. I held a wet towel in my hands and forgot to wipe the bar. When Ryan finally turned back to Simonakis, you could see he had made up his mind. He spoke slowly and carefully.

"Mr. Simonakis," he said.

The old man raised his head scowling.

"Mr. Simonakis," Ryan said. "Will you be kind enough to join my friends and me in a drink?"

The old man stopped scowling. He nodded gravely and stood up tall and straight, his mustache curved in dignity, and came to the bar. Ryan moved aside to make a place for him.

I began to pour the beer.

"No, George," Ryan said. "We will have wine this trip."

"Yes, sir," I said.

I took down the bottle of port and filled a row of small glasses.

Ryan raised his glass and looked belligerently at the others. "To the glory of Greece," he said.

The rest of them raised their glasses.

"To Athens," Sol said.

"To Mr. Simonakis," Olaf said.

"Ditto," Bernard said.

I took down another wineglass. I poured myself some wine. They all looked at me. I did not care. I was abandoning a professional tradition of neutrality.

"To Pericles," I said.

Simonakis stroked his mustache and sipped his wine. The rest of us sipped right with him.

THE MIRACLE

He was weary of tears and laughter. He felt perhaps he had been a priest too long. His despair had grown until it seemed, suddenly, bewilderingly, he was an entity, separate and alone. His days had become a burden.

The weddings and baptisms which once provided him with pleasure had become a diversion, one of the myriad knots upon the rope of his faith. A rope he was unable to unravel because for too long he had told himself that in God rested the final and reconciling truth of the mystery that was human life.

In the middle of the night the ring of the doorbell roused him from restless sleep. His housekeeper, old Mrs. Calchas, answered. Word was carried by a son or a daughter or a friend that an old man or an old woman was dying and the priest was needed for the last communion. He dressed wearily and took his bag and his book, a conductor on the train of death who no longer esteemed himself as a puncher of tickets.

He spent much time pondering what might have gone wrong. He thought it must be that he had been a priest too long. Words of solace and consolation spoken too often became tea bags returned to the pot too many times. Yet he still believed that love, all forms of love, represented the only real union with other human beings. Only in this way, in loving and being loved, could the enigmas be transcended and suffering be made bearable.

When he entered the priesthood forty years before, he drew upon the springs of love he had known. The warmth of his mother who embodied for him the home from which he came, bountiful nature and the earth. The stature of his father as the one who taught him, who showed him the road to the world. Even the fragmented recollection of the sensual love of a girl he had known as a boy helped to strengthen the bonds of his resolve. He would never have accepted his ordination if he did not feel that loving God and God's love for all mankind could not be separated. If he could not explain all the manifestations of this love, he could at least render its testaments in compassionate clarity.

But with increasing anguish his image seemed to have become disembodied from the source. He felt himself suddenly of little value to those who suffered. Because he knew this meant he was failing God in some improvident way, a wounding shame was added to his weariness.

Sometimes in the evening he stopped by the coffeehouse of Little Macedonia. There the shadows were cool and restful and the sharp aroma of brandies and virulent cigars exorcised melancholy for a little while. He sat with his old friend of many years, Barbaroulis, and they talked of life and death.

Barbaroulis was a grizzled and growling veteran of three wars and a thousand tumbled women. An unrepentant rake who counted his years of war and lechery well spent. An old man in the twilight of his life with all the fabled serenity of a saint.

"Hurry, old noose-collar," Barbaroulis said. "I am half a bottle of mastiha ahead."

"I long ago gave up hope of matching you in that category," the priest said.

Barbaroulis filled both their glasses with a flourish. "Tell me of birth and marriage and death," he said.

"I have baptized one, married two, and buried three this last week," the priest said.

Barbaroulis laughed mockingly. "What a delightful profession," he said. "A bookkeeper in the employ of God."

"And whose employ are you in?" the priest asked.

"I thought you knew," the old man said. "Can you not smell sulfur and brimstone in my presence?"

"An excuse for not bathing more often," the priest said.

"You are insolent," the old man growled. He called out in his harsh loud voice and a waiter exploded out of the shadows with another bottle of mastiha. Barbaroulis drew the cork and smelled the fragrance with a moan of pleasure. "The smell of mastiha and the smell of a lovely woman have much in common," he said. "And a full bottle is like a lovely woman before love."

"Your head and a sponge have much in common, too," the priest said. "Wine and women are ornaments and not pillars of life."

"Drink up, noose-collar," Barbaroulis said. "Save your sermons for Sunday."

The priest raised the glass to his lips and slowly sipped the strong tart liquid. It soothed his tongue and for a brief illusive moment eased his spirit. "The doctor has warned you about drinking," he said to Barbaroulis. "Yet you seem to be swilling more than ever before."

"When life must be reduced to an apothecary's measure," Barbaroulis snorted, "it is time to get out. I am not interested in remaining alive with somber kidneys and a placid liver. Let the graduate undertakers who get me marvel at my liver scarred like the surface of a withered peach and at my heart seared by a thousand loves like a hunk of meat in incredible heat."

"You are mad, old roué," the priest said. "But sometimes I see strange order in your madness."

"Even a madman would renounce this world," Barbaroulis said with contempt. "Why should anyone hesitate giving up the culture of the bomb and the electric chair? We are a boil on the rump of the universe and all our vaunted songs are mute farts in the darkness of eternity."

"You assemble the boil and the fart," the priest said, "from the condition of your liver and your heart."

"When will you admit, noose-collar," Barbaroulis laughed, "that the limousine of faith has a broken axle?"

"When you admit," the priest said, "that the hungry may eat fish without understanding the dark meaning in its eye." He finished his drink and rose regretfully to go.

"Leaving already?" Barbaroulis said. "You come and go like a robin after crumbs."

"There is a world outside these shadows," the priest said.

"Renounce it!" Barbaroulis said. "Forsake it! Join me here and we will both float to death on exultant kidneys."

"You are a saint," the priest said. "Saint Barbaroulis of the Holy Order of Mastiha. Your penance is to drink alone."

"What is your penance?"

The priest stood for a moment in the shadows and yearned to stay awhile longer. The taste of the mastiha was warm on his tongue and his weariness was eased in the fragrant dark. "Birth and marriage and death," he said and waved the old man goodby.

On Sunday mornings he rose before dawn and washed and dressed. He sat for a little while in his room and reviewed his sermon for the day. Then he walked the deserted streets to the church.

There was a serenity about the city at daybreak on Sunday, a quiet and restful calm before the turmoil of the new week. Only a prowling tomcat, fierce as Barbaroulis, paused to mark the sound of his steps in the silence. At the edge of the dark sky the first light glittered and suspended the earth between darkness and day.

The church was damp from the night and thick with shadows. In a few moments old Janco shuffled about lighting the big candles. The flames fingered flickers of light across the icons of the white bearded saints.

He prepared for the service. He broke the bread and poured the wine for the communion. Afterward he dressed slowly in his vestments and bound the layers and cords of cloth together. He passed behind the iconostasis and through a gap in the partition saw that the first parishioners were already in church awaiting the beginning of the service. First, the very old and infirm regarding the ornaments of God somberly and without joy. They would follow every word and gesture of the liturgy grimly. Their restless and uneasy fingers reflected the questions burning in their minds. Would the balance sheet of their lives permit them entry into the city of God? Was it ever too late to take solace in piety and assurance in sobriety?

After them the middle-aged entered. Men and women who had lived more than half their lives and whose grown children had little need for them anymore. Strange aches and pains assailed them and they were unable to dispel the dark awareness of time as enemy instead of friend.

Then the young married couples with babies squirming in their arms, babies whose shrill voices cried out like flutes on scattered islands. In the intervals when they were not soothing the infants, the young parents would proffer their devotions a little impatiently while making plans for the things to be done after church.

Finally the very young girls and boys, distraught and inattentive, secured to the benches by the eyelocks of stern parents. They had the arrogance of youth, the courage of innocence, and the security of good health.

When the service was over they all mingled together for a milling moment and then formed into lines to pass before him for bread. Old Janco began snuffing out the candles in the warm and drowsy church. The shadows returned garnished by incense. The church emptied slowly and the last voices echoed a mumble like the swell of a receding wave. In the end only he remained and with him the men and women standing in the rear of the darkened church waiting to see him alone.

"Father, my daughter is unmarried and pregnant. A boy in our neighborhood is guilty. I swear I will kill him if he does not marry her."

"Father, my husband drinks. For ten years he has promised to give it up. Sometimes there isn't money enough to buy food for the children's supper."

"Father, all day I look after my mother in her wheelchair. I cannot sleep at night because I dream of wishing her dead."

"Father, my child is losing his sight. The doctors say there is nothing that can be done."

"Father, ask God to have mercy on me. I have sinned with my brother's wife."

"Father, pray for me."

Until the last poor tormented soul was gone, and he stood alone in the dark and empty church. In the sky outside a bird passed trailing its winged and throaty cry. He knelt and prayed. He asked to be forgiven his sins of weariness and despair and to be strengthened against faltering and withdrawal. For a terrible instant he yearned for the restful sleep of death.

THERE WAS a night that summer when the doorbell rang long after midnight. He woke from a strange and disordered sleep to the somber voice of Mrs. Calchas. Barbaroulis was dying.

He dressed with trembling hands and went into the night. His friend lived in a rooming house a few blocks away and the landlady, a grim-faced Circe, let the priest in. She told him the doctor had come and gone. There was nothing more to be done.

Barbaroulis lay in an old iron-postered bed, a decayed giant on a quilt-and-cotton throne. When he turned his head at the sound of the door, the priest saw that dying had refashioned the flesh of his face, making the cheeks dark and tight and the eyes webbed and burning.

"I was expecting Death, the carrion crow," Barbaroulis said. "You enter much too softly."

"Did you wake me for nothing?" the priest said. "Is your ticket perhaps for some later train?"

Barbaroulis grinned, a twisting of flesh around his mouth, and the husks of his teeth glittered in the dim light. "I sent for you to get it," he said.

"Get what?"

"The bottle of mastiha," Barbaroulis said. "My mouth is parched for some mastiha."

"The custom is for communion," the priest said.

"Save it," Barbaroulis said. "There is a flask of mastiha in the corner behind the books. I have hidden it from that dragon who waits like a banshee for my wake."

The priest brought him the flask. The great nostrils of Barbaroulis twitched as he smelled the sharp aroma. He made a mighty effort to raise his head and the priest helped him. The touch of the old man's expiring flesh swept the priest with a mutilating grief. A little liquid dribbled down the old man's chin. Breathing harshly, he rested his head back against the pillow. "A shame to waste any," he said.

"Tomorrow I will bring a full bottle," the priest said, "and serve it to you out of the communion chalice. We might get away with it."

"Drink it yourself in my memory," Barbaroulis said. "I will not be here."

"Where is your courage?" the priest asked gruffly to cover emotion. "I have seen men sicker by far rise to dance in a week."

"No more dancing for Barbaroulis," the old man said slowly and the mocking rise and fall of his voice echoed from the hidden corners of the room. "The ball is over, the bottle empty, the strumpets asleep. Pack me a small bag for a short trip. Only the lightest of apparel."

"A suit of asbestos," the priest said.

"I have no regrets," Barbaroulis twisted his mouth in a weird grin. "I have burned the earth as I found it. And if word could be carried far and fast enough a thousand women would mourn for me and rip their petticoats in despair."

"Are you confessing?" the priest asked.

"Just remembering," Barbaroulis said and managed a sly wink. "When I see your God," he said, "shall I give him a message from you?"

"You won't have time," the priest said. "The layover between trains will be brief."

The old man's dark parched lips stirred against each other in silent laughter. "Old noose-collar," he said, "a comfort to the end."

"Saint Barbaroulis," the priest said. "The Holy Order of Mastiha."

"What a time we could have had," Barbaroulis said. "The two of us wenching and fighting and drinking. What a roisterer I could have made of you."

"What about you in church?" the priest said. "You might have become a trustee and passed the collection plate on Sunday. Who would have dared drop a slug before your fierce and vigilant eyes? Gregory of Nazianzus would have been a minor saint beside you."

Barbaroulis laughed again with a grating sound as if bone were being rubbed against bone. Then the laughter faltered and a long shudder swept his body. His fingers, stiff as claws, curled in frenzy upon the sheet.

The priest watched his terrible struggle and there was nothing he could do but grip the old man's hand tightly in his own.

Barbaroulis made a sign with his raging eyes and the priest moved closer quickly. A single moment had transformed the old man's face into a dark and teeming battleground of death. His lips stirred for a moment without sound and then he spoke in a low hoarse whisper and each word came bitten slowly from between his teeth.

"I have known a thousand men and women well," he drew a long fierce rasp of breath. "I have loved only one." His voice trailed away and the priest moved closer to his lips that trembled fiercely to finish. "A priest who reflects the face of his God."

Then his mouth opened wider and his teeth gleamed in

a jagged line. For a moment he seemed to be screaming in silence and then a short violent rush of air burst from his body.

The priest sat there for a long time. In death the old man seemed to have suddenly become half man, half statue, something between flesh and stone. Finally the priest rose and closed his eyes and bent and kissed his cheek.

He left the room. The street was black but the roofs of houses were white in the glow of the waning moon. A wind stirred the leaves of a solitary tree and then subsided.

His friend had been a man of strife and a man of contention. But into the darkness the old man had borne the priest's grief and his sorrow. In his final moment Barbaroulis had fed his loneliness and appeased his despair. And as he walked, he cried, and the great bursting tears of Lazarus ran like wild rivers down his cheeks.

COURTSHIP OF THE
BLUE WIDOW

SOMETHING HAPPENED to me the first time I saw the Widow
Angela in the grocery of old Mantaris. More than just the
restless stirring of flesh a man feels in the presence of a
lovely woman. I was bothered as I am often bothered
when I see a woman I like I cannot at once touch. After
she walked out with the bread and cheese she had bought,
I asked old Mantaris about her.

He rubbed his big knuckled fingers across the leathery
skin of his cheeks. He shook his head sadly. He drew a
long breath and sighed.

"She is a woman, that one," he said. "She was born and
reared in the mountains of the old country. A grown
woman at fourteen. She came to this country and married
a giant of a man who worked in produce. Then her man
died."

"How long has her man been dead?" I asked.

He shook his head slowly, trying to remember.

"Two years ago," he said. "Maybe a little longer. He was a Spartan. A big man with the arms of a wrestler. She has been in mourning ever since."

Two years and maybe longer. Too long for a woman built as the Widow Angela was built to set a seal upon her heart.

Then I understood what had bothered me about her. She was tall and dark with dark hair pinned back into a prim bun. Her face was pale and clean of powder or rouge. Her lips were full but untouched by lipstick. The black dress she wore was a plain dark folding of cloth high across her breasts and full across her thighs. She was without any of the artifices women use to point up their womanliness. In some strange way this made her more beautiful than any woman I had ever seen.

"She sleeps in a widow's bed," Mantaris said, and his voice shook with woe. "Her good husband sleeps in the cold earth." He paused and licked his thin dried lips. "I saw her once at a picnic with him some years ago. She danced in a line of women, taller than any other. That day she was not pale-cheeked as she is now but hot with life. Not one of your withered city women but a mountain woman wild with the flow of heroic blood."

"You are a patriarch now," I said. "A recorder of history and a recounter of legends. Stop bagging your bread and slicing your cheese long enough to advise me where she lives."

Suddenly one of his big long fingers pointed straight at my head like a gun. His leathery cheeks quivered and his eyes burned. "I know who you are," he said. "You are a Turk bent upon pillage and rape!" He clenched his fist and beat his chest. "You do not see the tragic nobleness of her grief. To see her now and remember her as she was hurts me here." He touched the region of his heart. His voice sharpened with contempt. "You are touched much further down."

"My friend," I said gently. "You do me an injustice. I too believe in the nobility of grief. Remember, I too am a Greek."

He shrugged and rippled noise through his lips. "It is true you are Greek," he said. "But there are Greeks and Greeks. Some are the descendants of lions, and others . . ."

I put my finger expectantly to my nose.

"Others come from goats," he said.

"She is a lovely woman," I said.

The hard lines of his face softened. "Yes . . ." he said. "Yes."

"A face like Helen to launch a thousand ships," I said.

He shook his head approvingly. "Yes," he said.

"She has breasts like great cabbages," I said.

He almost leaped to the ceiling. When he came down with his face flaming he slammed his open palm upon the counter. "Your head is a cabbage!" he yelled. "You have no respect!"

"You are right," I said. "My old dried-up friend, you are right."

He looked at me scornfully.

"What can you know," he said. "What can a young goat know of dignity and beauty?"

"A woman is going to waste while you call me names," I said. "I leave you to your cabbages."

"Then leave your head!" he shouted. "I'll weigh it with the rest."

I waved back from the door.

THE NEXT day was Sunday. All the night before I had tossed restlessly with dreams. I dreamed of the pale-faced

Widow Angela whose body looked long asleep. There were fine cabbages in my dreams and an old toothless lion who guarded the gate to the patch.

In the early morning I shaved carefully and dressed and left my rooms. I crossed the square past the closed stores. I went to the church beside the Legion hall. I waited outside. From within I could hear the full deep tones of the organ and the chanting of the priest.

I waited there until the services ended. Until the doors were opened and the first men and women came out. When I saw Mantaris I called to him. He looked about and blinked in the sunlight and then saw me and came closer.

"Watch for her," I said. "Watch for the widow."

He looked at me in shock and surprise. "You are a crazy man!" he said. "Is your head on straight or do I call for help?"

"If you don't introduce me," I said, "I will accost her myself, here in front of the church."

"You would not dare!" he said, and then breathing hard he shook his head slowly. "You would. You are part Turk."

Then I saw her and my fingers tightened again around his arm. She came out into the sunlight and the black dress she wore saddened my heart. She wore a small dark hat over her dark hair and her cheeks were still pale and she walked stiffly without notice of those who walked around her.

The old man trembled at my side.

"God help me," he said, and he crossed himself quickly and I gave him a little push and we started through the crowd. A short way down the stone steps we caught up to her and he called out her name and she stopped and turned. He looked around once more desperately as if thinking of escape and then spoke quickly. "Good morning, Mrs. Angela," he said. I stood close behind him, a somber look upon my cheeks. "It is a bright morning," he said.

"Good morning, Mr. Mantaris," she said. "Yes, it is a bright morning."

I punched the old man in the back and he jumped. "Mrs. Angela," he said, and he seemed to be having trouble getting the rest out. "May I present Mr. Larakis."

"How do you do, Mrs. Angela," I said, and I was very careful not to smile. One does not laugh before the watch fires of grief.

She looked from the old man to me and her face darkened slightly. The old man shifted in some sort of agony from one foot to the other. Then she nodded an acknowledgment slowly and turned to walk on.

I punched the old man in the ribs again to follow her. He turned on me snarling like he was going to take a chance and clout me. He would not budge. He stood like one of the pillars of the Parthenon. I left him spitting at me under his breath.

I had to run several steps to catch up to her. "Excuse me, Mrs. Angela," I said. "May I walk with you to the next corner? We are going the same way."

She turned again and looked at me darkly. I think what saved me was the cool and impersonal expression on my face. A shadow of a smile would have whipped me right there. She nodded without speaking and I fell into step beside her.

We walked silently for a little way and the cars passed in the street and the spring sun shone brightly in the sky.

"Forgive me, Mrs. Angela," I said. "I knew your husband. I was grieved when I heard of his death. I have been out of the city a long time."

She looked at me with those deep dark eyes and there

was nothing I could understand on her face. Then her cheeks loosened just a little. "Thank you," she said quietly. "It was a terrible loss."

I spoke softly and sympathetically. "A fine man," I said. "Did he ever wrestle? I do not remember ever seeing a man with stronger-looking arms."

She shook her head slowly. I was sorry for the remembered pain returned to her cheeks. I am not a sadist. But this initial surgery was necessary. "He was not a wrestler," she said. "But he was very strong."

"I believe he once mentioned to me he came from Sparta?" I said.

"Yes," she said. "Kostas was a Spartan."

"Of course," I said. "Where else? Sparta stands for strength and courage."

We had reached the corner and she stopped and looked at me again. "He would have been pleased to hear you say that," she said. "Thank you, Mr. . . ."

"Larakis," I said. "Mike Larakis."

"Thank you, Mr. Larakis," she said. "Now I turn here."

I took a deep breath. I had to proceed carefully. Whoso diggeth a pit might fall therein. "Mrs. Angela," I said. "Please do not think I am disrespectful. It is only I have not been back in the city very long. My old friends are moved and gone. Can you understand what it is to be lonely?"

That one was a beauty. I could see the shaft of the arrow sticking out of her wonderful chest.

"I know what loneliness is," she said. She spoke those words with real feeling.

I pushed my advantage. "Would it be too forward of me to think you might permit me to have dinner with you?" I asked. "Some quiet restaurant where we might sit and talk?"

She looked at me closely and I felt unrest under the intensity of her gaze. Those big dark eyes were more than ornaments on the Widow Angela. Her soul poured through them. "I do not go out socially," she said. "Not since my Kostas died."

"Forgive me," I said. "I was too forward. I have offended you. I am sorry."

I apologize very well. Frankly, it is not an easily acquired skill.

She shook her head. "Please," she said. "I was not offended. Just that it has been so long."

"A little food," I said. "A little quiet talk with a friend. Surely to allow yourself that is not to show disloyalty to a sacred memory."

I could see her making up her mind. Her skin without make-up gleamed cleanly. I felt a smarting in my fingers. Sweet is a grief well ended.

"All right," she said.

"Thank you," I said humbly. "You are kind to a lonely man." I paused and looked thoughtfully into space. This needed a clincher so she would not change her mind. "I regret I cannot make it tonight," I said. "There is a meeting of one of the church organizations I have just joined." I paused again. "I would rather sit and talk with you," I said.

"You must attend your meeting," she said firmly. "We will make it another night."

"Tomorrow night," I said. "If you are free."

"Tomorrow night," she said.

"I will call for you," I said. "Do you live close by?"

"The brownstone house," she said. "That one across the street. I have the first-floor apartment."

"At six?" I said.

"At six," she said.

"Thank you," I said.

She turned and walked away and I watched with intense interest the fine great sway of her marvelous thighs and savored my small pleasure like a general who had won the first skirmish but needed yet to win the war.

ON THE following afternoon I stopped for a moment in the grocery. Mantaris was bagging warm bread from the oven in back of the store. As I walked in he raised his head and sniffed as if an animal had entered.

"Good evening, old man," I said.

He stood glaring at me.

"I merely stopped by to let you know," I said. "Tonight I dine with the Widow Angela."

"You lie!" he said.

"This is a serious matter," I said. "I never lie where love is involved."

"Love!" The old man looked as if he might strangle on the word. "You would not know love if it had teeth and bit you in the ass."

"I will let that pass," I said. "Tonight I dine with a Queen and feel kindly toward the peasants."

"Get out, boofo!" he cried. "Go and drop dead!"

I left the store smiling and went home to dress.

At six that evening I rang the bell of the Widow Angela. She opened the door and she was ready and we said good evening to one another and commented on the fine spring weather. She went to put on her hat and came back and we walked down the stairs. I led her toward the car. She shook her head.

"Such a lovely evening," she said. "Let us walk. There is a little restaurant a few blocks from here that I often pass and have never entered. May we go there tonight?"

"Certainly," I said.

The restaurant she had spoken of was a small one off

Dart Street. A little bell rang over the door as we entered and we walked down a few stairs into a small room with a row of booths and candles on the tables. I could not have picked a better atmosphere myself.

A small dark man with a heavy mustache greeted us and ushered us to a booth. We sat down. I ordered a glass of wine. She hesitated, and finally nodded. We ordered another glass. I sat back and looked at her. Her face in the candled light of the booth was a page from an Old Testament psalm. David to Bathsheba. And Solomon's song.

"You are very kind," I said, "to take pity on a lonely man."

She shook her lovely head. "You must not say that," she said. "I have been lonely too. It was generous of you to ask."

I am fearfully and wonderfully made. I caused the Widow's heart to sing with joy.

"You are shy," she said. "I understood that yesterday when we walked from church. You must try to make friends."

I was trying to make friends. Angela, Angela, you have no idea how hard I was trying.

"I cannot help myself," I said. "As a child I was shy. I have never fully gotten over it."

The waiter brought the bottle of wine. He poured from it into our glasses. The wine gleamed dark red. "In wine there is truth," I said.

She raised the glass to her mouth. When she lowered it the stain of wine glittered wetly on her lips. "What is the truth?" she said.

"That you are lonely," I said. "That you mourn golden days that can never be again."

A sob seemed to catch in her throat. "Never again?" she said.

"Not in the same way," I hastened to add. "The past has its place. Memories remain sacred, but one must somehow live."

I filled her glass again with wine. For a girl out of circulation for over two years she knocked off that wine like a champion.

"There are nights I cannot sleep," she said. "Nights when I lie awake and hear strange noises in the dark."

"Loneliness," I said. "There is nothing more terrible than loneliness." As an alternative, Larakis offers himself as chosen comforter. Lucky Angela.

We ordered a little food. I poured another glass of wine. In a little while bright patches of red adorned her cheeks and her teeth gleamed even and white when she smiled.

"It seems so long ago," she said, "since I have sat like this and tasted wine and talked a little."

"You are still young," I said. "You have your life ahead of you."

"And you?" she said. "You are young and have known loneliness. Is your life still ahead of you?"

"For both of us," I said.

She paused and took another sip of wine and held her head a little to the side watching me intently. "I am glad," she said.

There was a bright spring moon high over the city as we walked home together past the houses and the stores and I did not even try to hold her hand.

After she had opened the door to her apartment she stood in the doorway weaving just a little. The scent of midnight tables was about her body. Aroma of walnuts, wine, and fruit. "Will you come in for coffee?" she asked. Her face was hidden in the shadows and I could not see her eyes.

I was tempted. But as an expert in such matters I knew

it was too soon. Timing in these things is the principal thing. Therefore if thou would emulate the master, get timing. And with all thy getting, get understanding.

"It is too late for you," I said. "You have been kind and I will not impose further upon your kindness."

"You are a good and gentle man," she said.

She was right. Only fools make a mock at sin.

"Tomorrow night?" I said.

"Tomorrow night," she said. She closed the door.

A WEEK passed. A week in which I saw the Widow Angela every night. Twice we ate in the little restaurant with the candles. Once we drove to an inn outside the city and ate beside a tree-shaded lake. Once we went to a movie and it was a sad love story and she cried. Several times after taking her home I stopped in for a little midnight coffee. She showed me an album of family photographs. She had been a remarkably well-developed child. In later photographs I could not help being a little glad that I was not conducting this raid for plunder while her husband was alive. He looked a real brute of a man. I had no doubts, however, of my ability to equal or surpass his capacities in the main event.

All that week I never once tried to touch the Widow Angela. Several times in the past few nights I had the feeling she would not have objected too strongly if I had kissed her good night. I refuse to match for pennies when a chance for a gold piece is involved.

Late Saturday afternoon it began to rain. I stopped in the grocery with two bottles of dark wine that were wrapped as gifts. Mantaris stared at the bottles.

"Won't be long now," I said.

He glared at me and pulled fiercely at his nose. "Why don't you leave her alone?" he said. "Why not a woman of the street or some other wench? Why the Widow Angela?"

"She is the Rose of Sharon," I said, "and the Lily of the Valley."

"You are a goat," he said. "You hold nothing sacred."

"You are a poor loser," I said.

"In the end you will give up," he said. "You will get nowhere with her."

"I will not give up," I said. "I am getting somewhere very fast."

"Get out!" he said. "You are a Turk! I spit back to your father's father!"

I looked around. "You have no fresh cabbages today?" I said.

He got red in the face and started to splutter.

"It does not matter," I said. "Tonight I think I pluck my own. Tonight, old man."

I heaped the coals of fire upon his head. He stood there and did not say another word.

On my way to the Widow it began to rain again. I ran from the car to the stairs making sure not to drop the wine. She stood smiling, waiting in the doorway. "Let me take your wet things," she said.

I gave her my raincoat and my hat. I carried the wine in myself. "A bad night," I said.

"It is very bad," she said.

"A good night to sit inside," I said. "The rain has chilled me."

She stood for a moment without answering and the light of the lamp shone across her face. Her lips were red with a touch of lipstick and there were marks of rouge upon her cheeks.

"I don't mind," she said.

She brought a corkscrew and little decorative glasses for

the wine. I opened one of the bottles. We sat together on the couch. We heard the whipping sound of wind and rain against the window.

"It has been a nice week," she said.

"I have enjoyed it very much," I said.

I refilled our glasses of wine. We sat without speaking for a little while with only our hands moving our glasses to our lips. The room seemed guarded like a valley between great mountains.

There was a record player in the corner. I got off the couch and walked to it and snapped the switch. The turntable revolved and the needle lowered upon a record. An old country mountain dance. Angela sat watching me from the couch.

"Come and dance," I said. "I have seen you dance before."

"Where?" she asked.

"At a picnic," I said. "You were taller than any woman in the line. You were beautiful and full of fire."

She stood up. The music rang the quick shrill melody. She came slowly to the machine. "I do not dance any more," she said.

"Why not?" I said.

"It is not right," she said.

I reached out and very gently touched the hair of the Widow Angela. I might have waited until she had more wine but I was not made of stone. Besides, there was something about that moment, something in the way she stood. I knew this was it.

She turned her head slightly and my hand fell away. For a moment I saw her face with the sad dark eyes and the full lips like moist fruit before a hungry man. "You must not touch me," she said.

I touched the nape of her neck, feeling the slight teasing softness of her hair across my fingers. "I want to touch you," I said, and I really meant that line. "Angela, Angela, all my body wants to touch you."

I saw the first press of uncertain breathing stir her breasts. She knew I had seen and the moment tightened under her disorder. "It is not right," she said. Her hand moved uneasily to her cheek. "It is not right that he should lie in the cold ground and that I should be warm and flushed."

"You are not dead," I said. "Angela, you are not dead. You are a living breathing woman. When you are dead you will be cold forever. Till then you must live."

She turned from me as I spoke. She stood with her back to me, her face to the wall, and her hair glistened darkly.

I snapped off the phonograph. The dance died sharply and a quick silence took its place. There was wild anticipation in my belly. I knew I had her then. I knew by the way she stood and would not look at me. Weeping may endure for a day, but Larakis cometh in the evening.

I reached for her and when she felt my hands she wantonly turned to meet me. I heard her breathing as if breathing were a punishment. Her eyes were closed and hollowed above her rouged cheeks and as I pulled her to me she opened them and they were frenzied and uncaring.

I kissed her full lips. My mouth hard upon her caught breath and the brazen scent of wine between us. The kiss broke and we shakenly drew breath and she stepped away for only a moment and then came back into my arms fiercely. I felt her fingers upon my face and on my throat and across my eyes. I quit goofing around. I started to pull her to the couch.

The buzzer rang a sharp shrill sound.

I felt her stiffen and I tried to catch my breath.

"We won't answer," I whispered. I caught her again. I reached for the great flowing hills of her breasts and felt them like fire beneath my hands.

Somebody pounded on the door.

We looked at each other. Her face, pale and shaken, reflecting my own.

"We must answer," she said huskily. She stepped away pulling weakly at her dress.

If I had had a gun in my hand at that moment I would have emptied it through the door without caring who it was. Instead I stumbled to it, cursing under my breath.

I flung it open and caught old Mantaris with his hand raised to pound again.

He looked startled and his mouth dropped open. The fierceness of my face must have scared blood out of him.

"What the hell do you want!" I roared.

He raised his hands in trembling defense. He stepped back and then looked around me quickly to where the Widow Angela stood. He spoke pleadingly to her watching me from the corner of his eye.

"Good evening, Mrs. Angela," he said and he reached down beside the door and brought up a large bag. "I am delivering your groceries."

I looked at him speechlessly. The Widow came closer to the door.

"Mr. Mantaris," she said, and her voice was still shaken. "I did not order any groceries."

The old man tried to look surprised and in his excitement and fear bounced up and down in the doorway.

"I was sure this was your order," he said. "Mrs. Angela, maybe you forgot about this order."

"Are you nuts?" I said, and a strange unrest bit at my belly. "She said she didn't order any groceries. Now get the hell away from here."

"Mike," the Widow Angela said reprovingly. She had regained her composure.

"I am very sorry, Mr. Mantaris," she said quietly. "There has been a mistake. I did not order any groceries."

The old man stopped bouncing and the sweat crouched in little beads across his brown cheeks and forehead. "I am sorry. I am getting old," he said. "I became mixed up. Forgive me."

For the first time I looked at the bag of groceries. I almost choked. Right on the top as bold as you goddam please was a cabbage! That did it. I gave him a shove and slammed the door in his face.

I turned back to the Widow. I was confused but not discouraged. I had come so close I refused to believe I could not make up the lost ground. I went for her again.

She greeted me with her elbows and a tight dark face.

"Angela," I said. "My darling, don't turn me away."

She shook her head. She stood like a stranger in the room. "It was wrong," she said. "If that old man had not accidentally come at the moment he did, it would have been wrong."

I watched her moist lips move as she talked and remembered them soft under my own.

"You can't go to bed alone forever," I said harshly.

She shook her head and her eyes were deep and clear. "Not forever," she said. "When I find a man to love and marry who will love me, we will go to bed."

I heard her with the hearing of my ear and saw her with the seeing of my eye. There was a roaring beginning in my head and a sense of outrage in my loins. "You are crazy," I said.

"I was for a little while," she said. "I am all right now."

"I won't give you up," I said.

"I will not see you," she said.

"I will make you see me," I said.

"We can be friends," she said.

That word nearly strangled me.

Her face was set into hard firm lines. She wore her virtue like a coat of armor.

I had enough. A man's heart deviseth his way but the Lord directeth his steps. While I was missing from the couch, the fire burned out.

"Goodby," she said.

I stood there a moment. Nimrod, the mighty hunter, returning with an empty pouch.

"My hat and coat," I said haughtily.

She turned to get them and I took one last mournful look at her strong fine thighs and the slender turn of her trim ankles. She brought me back my things. She walked to the door and opened it. I walked past her and turned in the doorway standing in the same place that sneaky old bastard had stood a few moments before.

"Angela," I said. "You are doing us both wrong."

She turned and walked out of the room and left me in the doorway with the door still open. If she had at least closed the door or pushed me out, but she left me standing there with the door still open.

With what dignity I could muster I reached in and closed the door in my own face. I turned and walked down the stairs.

In the car I debated between throwing a rock through the window of the Mantaris grocery or going to Crotty's bar. I decided on the bar. If I hurried I knew a cigarette girl there that I might talk into taking the night off. She had a squeaky giggle and an unfortunate tendency to cold feet, but any port in a storm.

An ass is beautiful to an ass and a pig to a pig.

To hell with the Widow Angela.

THE LEGACY OF LEONTIS

LEONTIS MARNAS married Angeliki when he was fifty-eight years old. She was twenty-four. She had been in the United States only a little over two years. All that time she spent working from dawn to dark in the house of an older brother who had paid her passage from Greece. Her days were endured scrubbing floors and caring for his children. In addition, the unhappy girl did not get along with her brother's wife, who was a sullen and unfriendly woman.

Leontis was not aware at that time of how desperately Angeliki wished for liberation from her bondage. When he visited the house in the evening to play cards with her brother, she released upon him all the smoldering embers of her despair. He would have been ashamed to admit that he mistook her attention for affection and her desperation for passion. He was bewildered and yet wished ardently to believe that a young and comely woman could find him attractive. He could not help being flattered and soon imagined that he was madly in love.

In the twenty-eight years since Leontis emigrated from Greece to the United States, he had made a number of attempts to marry. Several times he almost reached the altar, but in the end these efforts were always unsuccessful. Even when he was a young man the bold girls had frightened him, and the shy sweet girls to whom he was attracted lacked the aggressiveness to encourage him. He was without sufficient confidence to make the first move, and as a result always lost his chance.

Sometimes despair and restlessness drove him to women that he paid for affection. As he grew older, however, these visits became much more infrequent, and when he realized they burdened rather than satisfied him, he gave them up.

A year came when he was forced to concede to himself that he would never marry. This caused him a good deal of remorse and self-reproach, but secretly he was also relieved to be spared additional disappointment. His mother, of whom he often said, God rest her departed soul, had affirmed that keeping busy prevented melancholia. He became active in a Hellenic lodge and sponsored the education of several war orphans overseas. He rearranged all the stock in his grocery at least twice in each six months. On Sundays, the hardest day of the week for him to sustain, he rode the trolley from one end of the city to the other. He visited museums and spent many hours at the zoo. He was strangely drawn to the monkey house and quietly marveled at his apparent resemblance to one somber old male in a corner of a cage who seemed untouched by the climate of social amiability that prevailed all around him.

During the week, after closing the store in the evening, he sometimes played cards with fellow members of his lodge. In the beginning, this was his reason for visiting the house of Angeliki's brother. Afterwards, although it took a while to admit it to himself, he went only to see her.

Later, in remembering that time, Leontis often considered how ridiculous his conviction that Angeliki loved him
must have appeared to her brother. Perhaps he saw their
union as an answer to his concern for the future of his
sister. But whatever his reasons, her brother gave his approval and completed the alchemy created by the loneliness
of Leontis and Angeliki's wish for freedom.

In the early spring of that year, with the first buds breaking in slim green shoots upon the trees, Angeliki and Leontis were married. But it did not take long for the poor girl
to realize she had merely substituted one form of despair
for another. He could offer her every advantage but the
one of youth to match her own. Leontis knew she must
have considered him ancient and unattractive, but his
presence in the rooms in which she bathed and slept must
have created in her an awareness of her body, and perhaps
excited her as well. She could see that he admired and
adored her, and at the same time he could not blame her
impatience with his fumblings.

She could not comprehend how difficult it was for him
to value himself as participant in the act of love. He had
too long lived vicariously on the perimeter of life. Yet he
desired her fervently and made a valiant effort to play the
role of lover. On a number of occasions he did manage to
fulfill the functions expected of him. But Angeliki grew
petulant and bitter at his inadequacies and began to ridicule
his age and appearance. A day came when his own long-
suffering patience wore thin, and they exchanged hot and
furious words.

"You married me for my money!" he said, and he knew
that was not true, but anger selects its own truth.

"No." She laughed bitterly. "I married you because you
were young and handsome."

He felt the black bile of despair through his body, and

he was tempted to strike her but understood helplessly that she could not deny herself the release of some of her frustration.

"I married you because you were handsome!" she shrieked. "A Greek god with a golden body!"

"Enough," he said, and suddenly his anger was gone and he was only weary. He saw in that moment the absurdity of his delusion and how much more he was to blame than she.

He fled down the stairs. In the store, Thomas Sarris, the young man who worked for him, was stacking cans of coffee. Leontis was ashamed and wondered if Thomas had heard them quarreling.

Upstairs, Angeliki slammed a door, a loud and angry slam. Thomas Sarris pretended he did not hear.

THE FOLLOWING spring, a son was born to them. Through the months of Angeliki's pregnancy, observing her body curving incredibly into the shape of a pear, Leontis felt sure the doctor had made a mistake. For a long time he had accepted that he would never have a wife. The prospect of becoming a father had been additionally remote. Not until the moment in the hospital shortly after Angeliki returned from the delivery room was he able to accept the conception as real. He was shocked at the sight of her pale cheeks and her dark moist hair, combed stiffly, in the way of hair on a corpse. Fifty-nine years on earth without awareness of the struggle of birth had not prepared him for the emotion. He could not speak. A great tenderness for his young wife possessed him. He touched her cheeks softly and struggled vainly to find words to explain that he understood the ordeal she had endured alone.

When they brought the baby to Angeliki to be nursed, he was rooted with reverence and wonder. He had seen babies before, not quite as small and wrinkled, but that this baby should be a part of his flesh, a blossom of his passion, filled him with a wild strength. As if in some strange and secretive way he had cultivated a garden beyond the reaches of his own death.

Back at home, Angeliki was a devoted mother and cared diligently for the baby. She was dismayed and fretful at the disorderly abundance of affection Leontis showered upon the child. But he could not help himself. He worked in the store, and whether or not he was alone, a moment came when he was filled with an overwhelming longing to see his son. He would run up the stairs and burst through the kitchen into the room where the baby played. Angeliki would follow him, nagging fiercely, but he paid her no attention. He would bend over the baby and marvel at how beautiful he was. He would kiss the top of his soft head and kiss each of his tiny warm feet. The bell in the store rang endlessly.

Angeliki drove him finally from the room.

"You are mad! I will have you put away. You think of nothing but that baby. Your store, your wife—nothing matters. We will end up in the street!"

He kept a few feet ahead of her, and puffing heavily he hurried down the stairs.

A few weeks before the baby's first birthday they baptized him in the Greek Orthodox Church on Laramie Street. Leontis planned a gigantic party. He had several whole lambs roasted, and fifty gallons of wine, and forty trays of honey-nut sweets. He rented the large Masonic hall and invited almost all of the congregation of the church to attend. It was a wild and festive night, and everyone appeared to marvel at the way Leontis danced. Angeliki at last caught him in a corner.

"What an old fool! You will drop dead in the air. Everyone is laughing at you. They think you are crazy."

But full of wine and lamb and gratitude, Leontis just

smiled. He danced and sang for love of his son, and he did not care what others thought.

Now, in that month of his son's baptism, sleeplessness, which had troubled Leontis for years, grew worse. He lay wakeful and still beside Angeliki and stared into the dark, and sweats came, and chills, and strange forebodings rode his restless dreams. He went secretly to his friend Doctor Spiliotis. The old physician examined him silently and spoke without sugar off his square tongue.

"Have you made out a will? If not, go home and attend to it."

"I have a will made," Leontis said. "Thank you, old friend, for the advice."

"No thanks to me," the doctor said brusquely. "Thank that heart of yours, which has endured all the abuse you could heap upon it. Many men have weak hearts. They live long lives by taking care. You seem determined to leave as quickly as possible."

"I have lived a long time," Leontis said. "Looking back, it seems to me there is nothing but time."

The doctor looked down and stabbed fiercely with his hand through the air.

"I only treat physical ailments," he said. "They have specialists now for sickness of the mind. For aberrations of old men who marry strong young girls."

"You should have been a diplomat, old friend," Leontis said.

"Understand me, Leontis," the doctor said. "The time is past for jokes. Unless you go to bed at once and move very little for six months or a year, I do not think you have long to live."

In that moment, Leontis understood the tangled emotion a man feels who hears sentence of his death. At the same time, it seemed his decision was clear.

"Who will attend the store?" Leontis asked. "Who will walk my son in the park in the afternoons? Who will sit with my family in church on Sunday mornings?" He paused for breath. "And if I go to bed, can this insure I will live a long time?"

"We can be sure of nothing on this earth," the doctor said.

"Then I will wait in the way I wish," Leontis said.

"Get out," the doctor said, but the affection of their long friendship softened his words. "I will send you a wreath, a big one, fit for a horse. It will be inscribed 'Athenian Fool.' "

"Save your wreath for someone less fortunate," Leontis said. "I have lived long enough, and I have a son who will carry on my name."

With the knowledge of his impending death, a strange calm descended upon Leontis. Recalling his sixty-odd years as dispassionately as he could did not permit him any reason for garish grief. He knew that except for his son there was nothing in his life worthy of exultation or outrage.

He was certain of Angeliki as a devoted mother who would love and attend the child. To provide them with economic security in addition to the store, he had been purchasing bonds in considerable quantity for years. Therefore, only the possibility of Angeliki's remarriage to a man who might mistreat the child caused him anxiety.

He began carefully studying the clerk in his store, Thomas Sarris. A young man of strong build and pleasant manner. On a number of occasions, Leontis had noticed him discreetly admiring Angeliki when she entered the store. For an instant, the thought of Thomas Sarris or any man replacing him as father to his son brought a terrible pang to his body, but reason calmed him. Thomas was not wild, as were many of the young men. He did not wish to be more than a good grocer, but he worked hard

and would care for his own. He would know how to sweeten
a girl like Angeliki and remove the memory of her bitterness in marriage to an old man.

He spoke cautiously to Thomas one afternoon.

"How old are you, Thomas?"

"Twenty-eight," Thomas said.

"Twenty-eight," Leontis repeated, and kept busy bagging loaves of fresh bread so that Thomas would not notice
his agitation. "How is it you are not married yet? Many
young men are in a great hurry to marry these days."

Thomas easily swung a heavy sack of potatoes from the
floor to the counter.

"I have not found the right girl."

"Are you looking?" Leontis asked.

"I will be ready when I find her," Thomas said. "But I
am intent on getting myself established first. Get a store
of my own."

Leontis felt his pulse beat more quickly.

"Do you like this store?" he asked in what he felt was
a casual voice.

Thomas shook his head enthusiastically.

"A wonderful store," he said. "A fine business. I would
give anything to have one like it someday."

Leontis turned away so that Thomas would not see the
sly and pleased smile that he was sure showed on his face.

From that day he brought the baby and Angeliki and
Thomas together. He invited the young man to dinner
and afterwards encouraged him to play with the baby. He
was gratified when Thomas was gentle and tolerant with
the child. And the presence of the young man seemed to
act as a balm upon Angeliki. She spoke more softly and
laughed easily, and there was a strange sparkle in her eyes.
Sometimes, in the course of those evenings, it seemed to
Leontis that Angeliki and Thomas and the baby were the

family and he the intruder. Awareness of this jolted him, and forgetting for an instant that this was his design, he would flee with the child to another room. He would sit in the dark, holding the child tightly in his arms, and with the bitter knowledge of their separation roweling his flesh, he sometimes cried, softly, so that Angeliki and Thomas would not hear.

SUMMER passed and autumn swept brown crisp leaves along the streets beside the torn scraps of newspaper. In the morning, opening the store, Leontis felt the strange turning of the earth and endured the vision of the sun growing paler each day.

He knew that it was too late, but he suddenly took great care not to exert himself and called to Thomas to move even the smallest box. More and more often, he left the younger man alone in the store and spent most of the day upstairs with Angeliki and the baby. In the beginning she reproached him for neglecting the store, but after a while she seemed to sense his weariness and left him alone. He sat and watched her work about the rooms and listened to the baby make soft squealing sounds at play. Sometimes Angeliki brought him the baby to hold, and they would sit together by the window, looking out upon the winter street.

One afternoon when it rained and the dark heavy sky filled him with unrest, he spoke to her for the first time of what was in his mind.

"Angeliki," he said. "If I died, what would you do?"

She looked up and paused in sewing a button on the sweater of the baby.

"What is the matter with you?" she answered sharply. "What makes you talk of dying?"

"I am getting older," he said. "It should be considered."

"I will not listen to nonsense," she said.

"Would you marry again?" he asked. "I would want you to marry again."

She did not answer, but bent again over her sewing.

"Thomas is a fine young man," he said. "He works hard in the store. He is gentle with the baby. He would make a fine father and husband."

Angeliki snapped down her sewing.

"What nonsense is this?" she said impatiently. "I have better things to do than sit here and listen to you talk nonsense." She rose to leave the room, but a slight flush had entered her cheeks at mention of the young man.

THERE WAS a night he woke with a strange pain in his chest. He looked fearfully at the clock on the stand beside the bed, as if in some senseless way he hoped to arrest time. He was about to cry out, but the pain eased almost as quickly as it had come.

Later the baby cried in his sleep, a thin wail that echoed in the silent room. Angeliki got up and brought the child to their bed and placed him between them. In another moment, her breathing eased evenly again into sleep.

Leontis turned on his side and comforted the child and fell asleep with the warmth of the child within his arms. A noise within his body woke him. His eyes opened as if his eyelids were curtains on all of life. He cried out in despair.

Angeliki sat up in bed beside the baby.

"Leontis, what is the matter?"

He was bathed in a terrible sweat, and his heart seemed to be fluttering wings like a trapped bird to escape from the cage of his body.

"Leontis!" she cried. "Leontis!"

He knew he was dying. Not fear or anxiety, as he had

known many times in the past months, but knowledge, swift and real as if seared in flame across his flesh.

"Leontis!" she cried. "You must not die before you forgive me!"

He touched the baby's face. He felt his nose, small and warm, and his eyes, and the soft strands of his hair.

"Forgive me!" she shrieked. "Forgive me!"

Her hands were on his face and then they were lost within the crest of a mighty wave that tossed his body. He tried to hug the boy with all of his soul, and the last great swell exploded from his eyes.

THE BALLAD OF DAPHNE AND APOLLO

You WOULD not have thought, to look at him, that my
friend Apollo was a subject for tragedy. He had none of
the great mournfulness of countenance that must have
marked Macbeth and Oedipus. But calamity is not the
divine right of kings alone.

Apollo played the guitar in the tavern of Ali Pasha,
where I worked as a bartender. He was in his middle thirties and of average height. He appeared taller because he
had a lean and hard body and moved with the grace of a
flamenco dancer. He had strong white teeth that flashed
in a warm and engaging smile.

In the evening, when the tables in the tavern filled
with patrons, he would ascend the low platform in a corner
of the large room. He played bright Greek mountain dances
that made any feet but my swollen and aching ones itch
to leap into the air. He played bucolic love songs of Zakyn-

thos and Thessaly, and old-country island melodies that I remembered hearing as a boy.

Late at night as the smoke grew thicker and the mastiha ran freely down eager throats, a line of wild old men would rise to dance. They would circle and weave among the tables in a brisk Hassapiko or a martial Tsamiko that provided the leaders a chance for precarious leaps and hazardous jumps.

It was on an evening near the end of summer that Daphne first came to the tavern. She entered alone sometime after midnight wearing a raincoat and a strip of silk scarf across her head that she untied as she approached the bar. Her hair as it tumbled free was the rich black shade of fine Calamata olives.

"I would like to see the boss," she said in a husky voice.

I walked to the door at the end of the bar and called for Ali Pasha. In a moment he came lumbering out of the office. He had a great, gross body, the disposition of a hangman and a range of facial expression from bitter to bleak. He also fancied himself a bit of a rake and sported a handlebar mustache with curled and pomaded tips that he pulled fiercely when he grew excited.

"I'm looking for a job," the girl said.

"Only men serve the tables," Ali Pasha said brusquely. "The kitchen staff are men as well."

She swept her hair back impatiently with one hand, exposing a long jeweled earring glittering on her ear. "Do you take me for a kitchen flunky?" she asked. "I am a singer."

"A singer," Ali Pasha said, and a rude leer settled around his mouth. "Where have you sung?"

"Plenty of places," she said. "My last job was at George Spartan's in Cleveland and before that the Hellas in Detroit. Business improves wherever I sing."

He gave her a long, appraising look. She was a handsome

young woman with a certain sensual boldness that made me uneasy. He motioned her to a stool. "Sit there," he said. "I will listen to you in a minute."

He walked toward the platform where Apollo sat. I wiped the bar briskly with a cloth. "Would you like a mastiha?" I asked.

"Thanks."

I poured her a glass, which she raised to her lips and drank as swiftly as any man.

"Is that guitar player any good?" she asked.

"He plays a beautiful guitar," I said firmly. "When he plays the songs of the old country, he returns old men like me to our mountains and our islands."

"If he could just make you forget the brandy and cigar stink of places like this," she said with a taunting little laugh, "he would still be the best I have ever heard."

IN ANOTHER moment Ali Pasha returned with Apollo. "This is Apollo Gerakis," he said to the girl. "He plays the guitar for me." He motioned to Apollo. "This girl is a singer."

"Daphne," she said. "Daphne Callistos."

"Daphne," I said. "Apollo and Daphne." The old legend came to my mind.

"What's that?" Ali Pasha asked.

"Nothing," I said. There was no use explaining anything classical to him.

"I suppose we can use a singer," Apollo said as he looked carefully at the girl. "Can you sing the songs of Pontus and Epirus and Crete?"

"I know them all," Daphne said. "The lullabies and the love songs and the laments."

"One thing you should know," Apollo said. "The salary here is next to nothing. I exist on tips which are tossed into a box while I play. We would have to share what tips we get."

"I've worked that way before," Daphne said.

"Never mind salary and tips," Ali Pasha said. "Let's hear her sing first."

She gave him a final amused look and walked with Apollo toward the platform, removing her raincoat on the way. She was sheathed in a black dress that fitted her body tightly. Ali Pasha uttered a low, hoarse curse.

When they reached the platform, they stood talking a moment, and then Daphne moved alone into the beam of muted light. Apollo struck the first chords of a lament and the men at the tables quieted slowly.

A lament is a morose and melancholy song, and Apollo played them with feeling. But as she sang I had the strange sensation I was hearing a quality of despair I had never heard before. Her voice, haunting and mournful, led us down the path where the stream of woe pours into the river of lamentation. At the tables men stirred, and a wind of pleased muttering swept the room.

When she finished the lament, Apollo changed the tempo to the lilting melody of a festive mountain dance.

Daphne placed her hands on her hips and threw back her head, and her voice, suddenly bawdy and vibrant, assaulted the room. At one of the tables near the bar an old man sleeping off too much to drink raised his head like a startled bird. Her ardor paid homage to the woodland spirits of fertility and abandon. In such a way must the wild nymphs have sung in the festivals of Dionysus before the satyrs playing their pipes made of reeds.

When she finished, a storm of applause rose from the roomful of men. She walked with a careless insolence past the tables, and many called to her and blew her kisses. She came back to the bar, and Ali Pasha showed his teeth in hungry admiration. "You sing all right," he said grudgingly. "The truth is, I don't really need a singer. It is an expense I might not be able to afford."

In another moment Apollo joined them. "You are very good," he said.

"The boss doesn't think I'm good enough," she laughed.

"Never mind the lousy salary," Apollo said. "I think you will fill the box."

"Out of which you'll take your half," Ali Pasha snarled. He spoke to the girl with a crooked attempt at a winning smile. "If you want to work, you can start tomorrow night at eight."

She nodded calmly as if the outcome had never been in doubt. She turned to leave, and Ali Pasha spoke slyly. "A good-looking woman like you will be a pleasure to have around."

She looked at him as if her eyes were knives severing little hunks of his flesh and made a motion of good night to the rest of us as she pulled on her raincoat. We watched her as she walked to the door. Ali Pasha tugged fiercely and silently at the tips of his mustache, and walked back into the office.

I dimmed the lights in a signal to the customers that we were preparing to close. Apollo sat down on a stool at the bar.

"I wonder where she comes from?" he said slowly.

"She is from disaster," I said, "and on her way to catastrophe." Then, because he did not seem to be listening, I reached across the bar and shook his arm. "Forget her," I said. "Don't get involved with her."

"She is not all that brass she puts on," he said. "When she sings, she sets dreams to weeping. I remembered that it has been a long and lonely summer. I am tired of playing my songs alone." He pushed off the stool. "Hurry and clean up, Janco," he said. "I'll buy you a cup of coffee on the way home."

He walked toward the platform for his coat and guitar. I snapped off the lights above the bar. The waiters were beginning to clear the tables, and customers were moving in reluctant groups to the door. An old man who had been sleeping on his arms was disturbed by the clatter and moaned hoarsely.

"No more auditions tonight," I said in a vexed voice. "We don't need another singer."

AFTER Daphne started to sing in the tavern, business became much better almost at once. Ali Pasha, merciless in his greed, set up additional tables that barely left room for the cursing waiters to squeeze by.

When Daphne sang an unhappy ballad or a lament, she had the old men weeping for the grand days of their lost youth. When she sang a dancing song from Macedonia and suggestively rendered the lyrics of a shy man and his bold wife, the old men went wild with delight. When the graybeards finally rose to dance, they exhausted themselves to demonstrate their unflagging virility, and leaped off the floor like drunken and festive roosters.

Ali Pasha couldn't take his eyes off her. When she sang, he gripped the tips of his mustache in anguish. She held him off by a fury of blazing defiance in the same way she held off the countless other males who stampeded around her at the end of each evening. She provoked my grudging admiration in the ruthless way she cut them down.

But Apollo confused her. Against him she raised defenses that were not needed. He pursued her with a gentleness that was a source of wonder to her. Slowly, almost against her will, she must have felt herself drawn to him. Perhaps he stirred in her a memory long lost in the tide of dark days, a dream of fair love.

THERE WAS a day in the beginning of October when rain fell until evening and left a brief scent of freshened earth across the city. Late in the evening Apollo came looking for Daphne and seemed distressed. A while after that, one of the waiters relieved me at the bar, and I slipped out the kitchen door to smoke a cigar and get some fresh air.

Daphne called my name from the shadows.

"What are you doing out here?" I asked. "Apollo is looking for you."

"Let him look," she said defiantly. "He is as bad as all the rest."

"Is he?" I asked quietly. I sat down on a crate and with a sigh raised my burning feet to rest on another.

For a long moment she did not answer. I drew a cigar from my pocket and struck a match, and in the brief flare of light I saw her pale and weary face.

"Perhaps he is," she said. "Perhaps he isn't. But there are times when I am sick and tired of all men."

"The fate of a handsome woman," I said.

She laughed mockingly in the darkness. "I only feel comfortable with you, Janco," she said. "Why is that?"

"My arteries and my bad feet," I said wryly. "You sense correctly they have immobilized me for any pursuit."

She fell silent again. Above us the rain clouds had disappeared and the stars glittered.

"Wasn't Apollo the name of a god?" she said.

"He was the god of life and light," I said. "And he loved Daphne above all other women."

"I knew the story as a child," she said quietly, "I don't remember now except that it was sad."

"Daphne was the daughter of Peneus, the river god," I said. "Apollo was seized with love for her, but she yearned to keep her freedom. Many lovers sought her, but she spurned them all.

"Apollo loved her and longed to have her as his own. She sensed he was different from all the others, but she was afraid. She belonged to the unspoiled woods and to the untamed rivers. He followed her relentlessly and told her not to flee from him as a lamb flies before the wolf or a dove before the hawk. He was the god of song and the lyre and played a mighty melody of love."

"A guitar player," she said softly. "Playing a sweet and sad guitar."

"She tried not to listen to him," I said. "She was innocent of the meaning of love. But he would not let her alone. Her strength began to fail, and she called upon her father to aid her, to change her form, which had brought her into danger. Scarcely had she finished pleading when a stiffness seized all her limbs. Her hair became leaves, her arms became branches, her feet stuck fast in the ground as roots. Apollo touched the stem of the tree and felt her flesh tremble under the new bark. And he wept for his lost love. 'Since you cannot be mine,' he sang, 'I will wear you for my crown. I will decorate with you my harp and my lyre. My songs will make you immortal.'"

When I finished, she moved restlessly from the shadows and for an instant stood in the strip of light before the door. "The legend does not tell the truth," she said, and there was a black and bitter edge to her words. "Do not believe she fled because she was innocent and cared nothing for him. She fled because she had known many men and did not deserve the kind of love he offered. She knew if they loved each other they might both be destroyed."

"It is only a story that belongs to the past," I said

wearily. "A bit of foolishness for children and old men."
She went in the door, and after a moment I followed.

IT WAS not long after that night that Apollo and Daphne
became lovers. I do not know why she changed her mind.
Perhaps even the daughters of gods have moments of
mortal yearning. And the legend does not tell us whether
in that unhappy chase the two of them did not pause for
a moment together, perhaps in an hour of twilight when
the darkening of the woods made them feel keenly the
burden of being alone.

No one told me they became lovers, but I knew by the
radiance that came from them when they were together.
Sometimes when they had finished their last song after
midnight they came to the bar, and I served them little
glasses of wine.

"Is she not beautiful, Janco?" he said, and there was
the intimacy of possession in the way his fingers touched
her hair. She accepted his touch, and I saw their faces stir
with the soft wind of each other's desire.

"Is he not mad?" she said and laughed her husky
laugh, animated and deepened by affection.

"He is a guitar player," I smiled. "You are a singer of
sad love songs. This gives you both a head start on madness."

"When I was a boy," Apollo said softly, looking at
Daphne, "I had dreams of conquering cities and of ruling
men. Dreams of loving countless fair and dark women."
He paused, and the words came shaken from his throat.
"I have found them all," he said. "In my love I have
conquered cities and rule all other men. In my love I have
spanned the oceans and circled the earth. In my love I
possess countless fair and dark women."

"He is mad," Daphne said, and in her eyes there was a

fierce longing to believe him. "He is trying to make me as mad as he is."

"The mad are sane," I said, "and the sane are mad. Only love can harness both."

She raised her glass of wine and watched me as she spoke. "Legends are stories that belong to the past," she said, and a shadow swept her cheeks. "Is that not true, Janco?"

"That is true," I said quickly. "A bit of foolishness for children and old men."

She accepted my assurance recklessly and held tightly to Apollo's hand. "Then I drink to the future," she said fiercely. "A future that will make stories of its own."

"I drink to that," I said and spoke from my heart.

I AM SURE the ugly trouble began with Ali Pasha. When he could not have Daphne, his soul festered in rancor and wished to destroy that which he had been denied, He whispered in low malevolent tones to the waiters, falling silent when I came near. They followed his dark spoor and, like coyotes that feed on what the wolf brings down, added their own venom to the pot. Rumors and suspicions and whispers about Daphne and her past spread furiously through the tavern. There were sidelong smirks and muted laughter when Apollo passed the tables.

When he understood something of what was going on, he twisted in frustration and rage, but could find no adversary visible. I think he wished mainly to protect and defend her, and yet the baleful laughter nourished disorder. He knew that the shadows of her past concealed much he did not relish, and he began to brood over what could not be forgotten.

I fought to help him where I could and yet protected Ali Pasha as well. I knew that if Apollo suspected the origin of the vile whispering there would be violence. Ali Pasha kept a loaded gun in the top drawer of his desk and was coward enough to use it if he were attacked.

Under the taunt of these aggravations Apollo one night flung a patron violently from the platform when he sought to slip a folded bill into a pocket of Daphne's dress. There was a roar of catcalls and jeers. The man who had been shoved shrieked for the police. Ali Pasha hurried him into his office to conciliate him. A moment later Apollo came raging to the bar, followed by Daphne.

"He meant nothing," Daphne pleaded to calm him. "That was a good tip, and he meant no harm."

"Let him choke on his good tip!" Apollo said. "I should have smashed him. I saw him paw you. I should have smashed the pig!" He twisted on the stool, all the weeks of provocation and helplessness fused into explosive direction. "I have to sit there and watch them hour after hour," he said. "Drunken pigs who think their grimy dollar entitles them any liberty."

"Listen, please," Daphne said in a low, soothing voice. "I can tell when one is a bad apple. I would slap that kind down myself. Mostly they are old roosters with cut claws showing off for applause from their friends. They mean no harm."

"They harm me!" Apollo said. "I do not want the woman I love pawed by pigs!"

Her eyes began to flash fire of their own. "You forget one thing," she said. "I am a singer of bawdy songs in a tavern. In Cleveland and Detroit I earned my tips this way. This is the way I earn my bread."

"To hell with that," Apollo said, and his cheeks shook off heat. "To hell with earning your bread that way."

"Don't tell me how to earn my bread," she said, and

the words came bitten from between her teeth. "From the time I was ten no one cared whether I had bread at all. I have made my own way and asked no favors and earned my bread. Don't tell me now what is right. Don't sit in judgment like a god over my life."

"What kind of woman are you?" he asked savagely. "Not to mind being pawed by a hundred men!"

She stepped back as if he had struck her. Then, without another word, she turned quickly and almost ran to the door. He made a sudden frantic motion with his hand to call her back and then changed his mind.

"Go after her," I said quietly. "You were not fair, Apollo. She cares a great deal for you. Don't let her grieve alone!" I looked uneasily at the closed door to the office. "Ali Pasha will be out in a minute."

"To hell with him," Apollo said. But the circles of anger around his mouth loosened slightly, and then he slipped off the stool and started after Daphne.

A moment later Ali Pasha came out of the office embracing the patron whose outrage seemed to have softened. "Give this gentleman two bottles of mastiha." Ali Pasha's voice dripped unctuous tones. "Drink them, sir, with my compliments."

After the mollified rooster walked away clutching his bottles, Ali Pasha quickly dropped the mask of civility. "Mark that down," he snarled. "Those two bottles come out of the guitar player's tips. Charge him the retail price." He glared around the room. "Where are he and the girl?"

"Out for the air," I said.

"You tell them when they get back," he said, spitting the words from beneath his flaring mustache. "You tell lover boy that one more outburst like that and he and his prize paramour can both clear out." The sweat glistened on his swarthy face. "Who the devil does he think he is to protect that tart?"

"He is only a man in love," I said slowly. "A poor man goaded and tormented by dirty rumors and vicious lies spread by animals who only feel at home in the dark."

The blood left his face as if I had struck him.

NOVEMBER came, and the hours of daylight grew shorter. Dusk and dark advanced as the winter nights closed down. For the first time that I could remember I dreaded the coming of winter. The bleakness of the earth mirrored a desolation gathering in myself. I tried to validate this as the ominous premonition of an old man who did not have long to live, but I knew it was really because of my grief and despair for Apollo and Daphne.

The ugly whispering and mocking laughter had slowly faded away. Even Ali Pasha tired of the brutal game. But the baleful harm had been done.

Apollo could not forgive or forget the measure of mockery Daphne and he had endured. He tasted a bitter cup of brooding that would not let him rest. Each night that Daphne sang he devised in fury that the room secreted her former lovers, and he held himself tense and ready for violence. She sought to soothe and reassure him, but he was beyond reason. When they could bear no more, they raged loudly at each other and did not care who heard. At other times they fought in a dreadful silence.

In those dissembled moments when they sought to tear from the fabric of the nightmare a pattern for survival, they drew me with frenzied gaiety into their plans.

"Can you see me tending house?" she asked, and laughed a quick, shrill laugh. "Janco, can you honestly see me in an apron?"

"I see you clearly," Apollo said. "I will come home weary in the evening—"

"And Daphne will greet you with a song and a dance," I said, smiling.

"She will greet me with a tableful of food," he cried. "Roast chicken and white pilaf and salad garnished with Calamata olives and ripe mezithra cheese."

"Where will this splendid meal come from?" Daphne asked.

"You will cook it," Apollo said. "As my mother cooked for my father."

"Fine," Daphne said mirthfully. "I will cook for you as your mother cooked for your father. Fine."

"You will cook it," Apollo spoke with confidence. "And we will invite Janco to dinner several nights a week."

"I will work hard to learn," Daphne said. "You might both be surprised at how good a cook I become."

"I think you will become a fine cook," I cried. "And when you achieve this mastery, Apollo will create a ballad about your prowess in the kitchen."

THERE WERE those other bleak and furious moments when he stormed past the bar into the office, and she followed as if she were tied to his flesh. I could hear their voices through the thin panels of wood.

"You are a madman," she told him. "You are blind and mad."

"I see enough," his voice trembled. "The way that sailor looked at you. The things you promised when you sang to him."

"It is only you I care about," she cried. "Don't you understand that?"

"You knew him from before," he said.

"I have never seen him before tonight."

"You lie!" he said savagely.

"I'm not lying!" she said. "I'm not lying!"

"There were other men," he said. "You cannot deny there were many other men."

"What can I say about that now?" she said, and a terrible pain rang in her words. "What can I do about that now?"

There was a day in the beginning of December when I got to the tavern very early in the afternoon and found it deserted except for Daphne on a stool at the bar.

"You are hours early," I said smiling. "Are you that attached to this place?"

"I am leaving, Janco," she said quietly. "I came to say goodby."

I could not answer. A sadness settled upon me. After a while I said, "Where will you go?"

"I don't know," she said. "I don't care."

"He will follow you," I said. "He will not let you go."

She did not answer or move for a long moment. Then she slipped off the stool and turned and stared gravely across the shadowed room with the chairs piled upon the empty wooden tables. "These places are all alike," she said bitterly. "When you have sung in one you have sung in all. They are graveyards one moment and circuses the next moment. They all have the smell of damp cellars that never see the sun."

"If you went away for a little while," I said. "For just a little while and then came back."

"That would do no good," she said. "You know that."

She walked a few steps, and her shadow rose and swept along the wall behind her as if seeking a place to rest.

"In the world outside," she said, "there are countless people who love and marry and bear children. They live one day like the next. I have never envied them before." A stricken wonder came into her voice. "I try to remember the moment for me when there was no turning back. I try to remember the moment such a dream was lost to me forever. I cannot." She shook her head wearily. "All my life seems a long, bawdy song."

She came slowly to where I stood and kissed me. Her lips were cold against my cheek. "I could not say goodby to him," she said. "I say goodby to you instead."

"Will you leave him a letter?" I asked. "A message?"

"Everything has been done." She shook her head. "Everything has been said." She walked toward the door of the office. "I will fix my face and go," she said. "The first waiters may come soon."

She stood for a moment in the doorway. Her face, suddenly stained with tears, had imperfections, but no face is faultless, and if grief and despair make any face ugly, still she glittered in that moment with some strange beauty. "So the legend is right in the end," she said. "Daphne and Apollo are lost to each other."

"Not really lost," I said. "They have loved each other. He will never forget her. He will wear her love for his crown and will decorate with her memory his harp and his lyre."

"You are a foolish old man," she said softly. "Life to you is a song and a harp and stories that belong to the past."

She closed the door behind her. I turned wearily to prepare for the evening, trying to ease my distress in the movements of habit, the opening of bottles and the wiping of glasses. A few moments later I heard the sound of a shot.

A cold wind from the grave swept my body, and I went quickly through the door to the office. She was sitting in an armchair with her head limply to one side and the tumbled waves of her lovely hair almost hiding her face. There was a small stain of blood on her breast above her heart and at her feet the gun of Ali Pasha from his drawer.

I made my cross and closed my eyes for a moment and cried out then, a terrible cry from the marrow of my bone, for Daphne and Apollo and for the earth which had lost their love.

THE WINTER seems to last forever. March is still a cold and dreary month. Sometimes the snow falls softly during the night, and in the morning the earth is frozen and buried. I walk shivering to work, and when I breathe, a quivering mist rises like smoke from my mouth.

The tavern is not the same. Ali Pasha carries a dark burden of guilt and drinks savagely and alone. The wild old men still dance, but without the vigor they had before, as if they are only sad and futile ghosts. Apollo still plays the guitar, but he is changed as well.

Many come to hear him play in the evening. I swear there are tears off his strings, and his songs are great white stars that set dreams to weeping. And as I stand behind the bar late at night and listen, it seems to me that I am back in the mountains of the old country under Homer's glittering moon. Parnassus stands behind dark mountains. The olive groves and the ruins of columns lie among the age-old trees. The sea and Piraeus are white with light. Under the stars the shepherds sleep beside their flocks.

When I have to sit down because my ankles are swollen and my feet hurt, I return unwillingly to reality and know I am only an old man. A foolish old man to whom life is a song and a harp and a legend that will never die.

PA AND THE SAD TURKEYS

SOME DAMN fool once said that all a Greek had to do to make money in a restaurant was to enter partnership with another Greek and watch the cash register. The guy that started that rumor better stay away from my Pa.

Our place wasn't classy enough to be called a restaurant. It was a drab lunchroom in a factory district near the railroad yards. We had six tables and twenty-six stools. They were all filled for an hour over lunch, and the rest of the day and night a customer might think the place was a graveyard.

There were three of us as partners, and that was a mistake. Pa and Uncle Louie had been partners for a number of years. When the army drafted me, Pa forgave me for having left college after one year, and, in a flurry of patriotism, he and Uncle Louie cut me in for an equal share of the business. They wanted me to have something to come back to a few years later. When I returned in a month with a medical discharge for a bad knee, Pa was sorry, but by then the papers had been signed.

Not that I wanted to stay in the lunchroom forever, but I was still developing my character and had nothing special that I wanted to do yet besides make a fortune playing the horses. The lunchroom was near a reputable bookie, and I had to spend the time between races somewhere. I worked out in front as a waiter, and Pa and Uncle Louie worked in the kitchen as chefs, dishwashers, butchers, and anything else that came up.

Business was terrible and getting worse. About three in the afternoon, when we hadn't seen a customer in two hours, Pa would stamp out of the kitchen and begin. "May the fiend that sold us this place fall in a sewer," Pa said. "May his back swell with boils and his lying tongue turn black."

"Take it easy, Pa," I said. "That won't bring in any business."

Uncle Louie came to stand smiling in the kitchen doorway. He and Pa were brothers, but they weren't a bit alike. Pa was big with a barrel back and the thick neck of a bull. A heavy head of hair, iron-gray at the temples, came down over his forehead until it almost merged with his bushy eyebrows. I loved him, but I had to admit he resembled a gorilla, with a disposition to match.

Uncle Louie was an amiable idiot. I don't say that with any intended disrespect. I loved him too. He was a good-natured gentle little man who always smiled. That might seem commendable except that Uncle Louie carried smiling too far. Tell him about a terrible auto accident with the occupants smashed and bleeding, and Uncle Louie would listen carefully and smile and shake his head. Working with Pa in the kitchen would have driven a normal man crazy. Uncle Louie was insulated.

Pa fixed me with a baleful eye. "Lucky for me you went one year to college," he said. "Tell me, how did you manage four years of education in that one year?"

Uncle Louie smiled broadly.

"Cut it out, Pa," I said.

"Sure," he said and shook his head violently. "I will cut it out when you stop playing the horses and start thinking of a way to save us. This place is a graveyard. You hear me, hoodlum, a graveyard, and you are standing around with a shovel."

"Shut up, Pa," I said. "Here comes a customer."

Pa stared in disbelief as a leather-jacketed baggage handler shuffled in the door and sat down at the counter. Uncle Louie scurried back to the kitchen.

I brought the customer a glass of water. Pa elbowed me aside and handed him a menu.

"Coffee," the man said.

For a moment Pa's face twisted in a silent snarl.

"With or without a toothpick?" Pa asked, and he stood above the man with his hairy arms spread wide on his hips. The man looked up as if suspecting a joke, but Pa was grim.

"Have you had lunch?" Pa asked.

The man gaped at Pa for a moment and then numbly shook his head.

"What are you waiting for?" Pa said. "By skipping a meal you do injury to your stomach. Regular eating habits assure a sound body." He shook his head sadly. "Your appearance is unhealthy. When did you last see a doctor?"

The man nearly fell off his stool in shock and outrage. He stumbled to the door and, with his hand on the knob, turned and spoke in choked indignation. "You must be nuts!"

The door slammed behind him.

"Nice going, Pa," I said. "That should help pick up business."

Uncle Louie stuck his head out the kitchen door. "Thomas," he said to Pa. "I was waiting to hear an order. Where is the patron?"

"Coffee!" Pa said. "At a time when I am faced with eviction for nonpayment of rent, that lout comes in and orders coffee."

"He doesn't care about our troubles," I said.

"Who does?" Pa said and laughed in a show of frivolity. "Does my horse-playing son care? My educated son who spent one hard year in college and got a degree in the Daily Triple."

"The Daily Double, Pa," I said patiently. "Get it right."

"Thank you," Pa said. "I am happy you are around to correct me. I am so happy I wish I could die now in the middle of my joy."

"Don't expire yet, Pa," I said. "The Oscar Mayer man is due in for the meat order for next week."

"No order," Pa said somberly. "They have refused us further credit unless we put up cash. Not a bone without money."

"I'm sorry, Pa," I said. "I'm broke."

Uncle Louie ducked into the kitchen. He might have been simple, but he knew when to disappear. Not that he had any money either, but he didn't want to put Pa to the trouble of asking.

Pa laughed again without mirth. "In this way does it end," he said. "Next week my doors will close for good. People will whisper all across the city that Thomas Lanaras has failed. The icebox has nothing left but three small pork chops."

"One chop left, Pa," I said apologetically. "I got hungry late last night."

He fixed cold furious eyes on me.

"Can't we have a macaroni and spaghetti festival next week?" I asked.

"Do me a favor," he said slowly. "Don't think. Don't talk. Don't make a suggestion." He walked stiffly to the kitchen. In a moment I heard him wailing to Uncle Louie.

SAM ANASTIS came in about four-thirty. He was a renegade wholesale meatman specializing in animals that died natural deaths. He had the wide hot smile of a professional con man, a high-pitched shrill voice, and he always looked back over his shoulder at intervals as if afraid he was being followed. He carried a brown bag that he held tightly as if it contained some peerless treasure.

I lifted my nose out of the racing form. "Pa," I called out. "Sam Anastis is here."

"Tell him to drop dead," Pa shouted from the kitchen.

Sam Anastis laughed heartily. "What a sense of humor that man has," he said brightly.

"He's a riot all right," I said.

Sam Anastis walked on small quick feet to the swinging door and opened it a little. "Mr. Lanaras," he called out gaily. "It is me, Sam Anastis. I want to talk to you."

"Go to hell, Sam Anastis!" Pa roared.

Sam Anastis laughed shrilly. When he could catch his breath he shook his head at me. "What a man," he said. "Always kidding."

He opened the door slightly again. "Mr. Lanaras, please come out now," he said. "Sam Anastis has something for you at a price. I could have sold to any of a hundred restaurants, but when this golden opportunity came my way, I thought of you."

Pa said something shocking in Greek that called in question the parentage of Sam Anastis.

"All right, sir," Sam Anastis grinned slyly. "All right. I'll have to take my proposition to Mr. Botilakis. How he will laugh when I tell him I offered it to you first."

He finished and stepped back quickly. A moment later Pa came violently through the swinging door. Uncle Louie followed smiling behind him. If there was anything could set Pa's teeth on edge, it was mention of our archcompetitor, the Olympia Lunchroom on 15th Street, run by that blackhearted Macedonian, Antonio Botilakis.

Pa pointed a big warning finger at Sam Anastis. "I give you thirty seconds," he said. "At the end of that time I personally will kick you from here into the gutter. Now begin!"

Sam Anastis wasted ten seconds trying to decide whether Pa was serious. When he realized Pa was, he hastily opened the bag he carried and drew out something long and scrawny. "Look!" he said triumphantly. "Look!"

"In God's name, what is it?" Pa asked.

Sam Anastis looked hurt. He appealed to Uncle Louie. "You know what it is, of course."

Uncle Louie furrowed his brow. He smiled sympathetically at Sam Anastis. "It looks familiar," Uncle Louie said brightly.

Sam Anastis looked heartbroken. "It is a turkey," he said. "A genuine milk-fed purebred turkey. A wonderful specimen."

"Of course," Uncle Louie said. "A turkey."

Pa looked incredulous.

"That is a turkey?" he asked.

"It is some kind of bird all right," I said. "I think I can make out a wing."

Sam Anastis laughed, and Uncle Louie laughed with him.

"Like father like son," Sam Anastis said. "Both always clowning."

"If that is a turkey," Pa said somberly, "it has been hit by a truck."

"No!" Sam Anastis exploded in protest.

"Why is it so dark?" I asked.

"I'm glad you asked," Sam Anastis said. "This turkey was raised on a farm in Florida. Healthy sunshine all year round."

He made off to hand the bird to me.

"I don't want to touch it," I said. "I don't want to catch whatever it was that killed it."

"I was in Florida once," Uncle Louie said.

"Sam Anastis," Pa said, "I have known you for ten years. I knew your father. In the old country he was arrested three times for trying to sell the Parthenon to tourists. For you to come in here and suggest I buy that bird is an action so arrogant even he would not have dared."

"What is the matter with this turkey?" Sam Anastis asked in a grieved voice.

"What did the autopsy show?" I asked.

"In Florida it was very pleasant," Uncle Louie said. "I spent much time on the beach."

"Get out," Pa said, and he waved his big fist toward the door. "Go sell that abomination to Botilakis."

Sam Anastis backed toward the door still dangling the turkey.

"You are making a terrible mistake," he said shrilly. "I have a crate of these fine birds. You can have them for twelve cents a pound. At twelve cents a pound your profit will be enormous."

Pa stopped short. "Twelve cents a pound?" he asked.

"We stayed at a big hotel," Uncle Louie said. He smiled warmly. "The windows looked out on the water."

"Pa," I said warningly. "Forget it. Serve those birds and the police will put us away for life."

Sam Anastis took a step forward.

"Any chef can fix an attractive bird," he whined eagerly. "These birds are a real test. A lot of boiling to tenderize the meat. Plenty of seasoning to lend aroma. A good thick gravy. Believe me, these birds are a challenge I would be proud to accept if I were a chef."

"Get out, Sam Anastis," I said. "I'm only a sad horse player, not a murderer."

"Wait," Pa said. "Let me examine that bird more closely."

"A turkey," Uncle Louie said. "Of course."

Pa took the bird and turned his nose away. He pressed the bony thigh. "There is meat there," he said. "And there. And there. There is considerable meat on it."

"What did I say?" Sam Anastis shrieked. "A lovely bird and for the price a steal. I make nothing on the sale, but I hope to keep you as friends always."

"How much will the crate come to?" Pa asked.

"Eighty pounds," Sam Anastis said quickly. "Exactly nine dollars and sixty cents."

"I'll give you seven-fifty," Pa said.

"I contracted for twelve cents a pound," Sam Anastis said, outraged. "I gave you the best possible price. I saved them for you. Now you make a ridiculous offer."

Pa shrugged. "Forget it," he said and turned away.

"Wait!" Sam Anastis cried. "It has been a long day. My feet hurt. I'll take it."

He started quickly to his car to get the turkeys before Pa changed his mind.

"Pa," I said. "You must be nuts. Poisoning people is no joke."

"Shut your face about poison," Pa said. "This is a miracle which has been provided to save us from bankruptcy and disgrace."

"Maybe they will let you work in the prison kitchen," I said.

"Zipper your mouth!" Pa said. "You have no faith. Uncle Louie and I will fix those birds. We will fix them so they would be fit to serve on the table of a king."

Sam Anastis came in struggling with the crate.

"Where?" he gasped.

"In the kitchen," Pa said, and there was a wild gleam in his eyes.

THAT NIGHT after closing, the lights blazed in our kitchen. Pa and Uncle Louie placed great pots of water to boil on the stoves. When the kitchen was shrouded in steam, they threw in the turkeys. They boiled them all night, the two of them fretting around the pots like a pair of mad chefs. The smell was awful.

On Saturday morning it was hard to get an order out of the kitchen because Pa and Uncle Louie were working frantically over those birds. Some of the smell from the night before still lingered, and when customers wrinkled up their noses and complained, I told them a gas line had broken.

We did a light lunch business because it was Saturday, and then the place emptied again. By sometime that afternoon the first batch of turkeys had been out of the ovens a couple of hours and the second batch was in. Pa came out and sat at one of the tables with a pad of paper and a pencil, mumbling to himself as he figured out the menus for the coming week.

"Monday will be roast young tom turkey," Pa said. "Tuesday, turkey and noodles. Wednesday, hot turkey sandwich. Thursday, chicken à la king. Friday, turkey hash." He finished pleased at his sagacity.

"You forgot chicken croquettes," I said.

"Shut up," Pa said.

I buried my head back in the racing form and wondered how I might sneak out to make a bet in the fifth race at Tropical Park.

Everything was quiet. No other sound than Pa mumbling and a mail truck rumbling past in the street outside. I heard the swinging door from the kitchen, and I looked up.

"Pa, look!" I said. "Look!"

Uncle Louie stood in the doorway. For the first time I could remember he wasn't smiling. There was a look of incredible distress on his face, and he held his hand across his stomach.

"Louie, what is the matter?" Pa asked.

Uncle Louie tried to speak, but no sound came. Before our eyes his face seemed to darken and his cheeks seemed to swell. He made another valiant effort to speak, and only a deep mournful croak came out.

"Louie!" Pa hollered. "In God's name, what has happened?"

"Pa!" I shouted. "I bet he ate some turkey!"

When he heard the word "turkey," Uncle Louie stiffened as if he had been shot. Then he stepped forward, placing one foot down carefully, and followed it slowly with the other. He made one final mighty effort to smile. When that failed he spun around like a top, once, twice, propelled by some relentless force, and then he collapsed on the floor flat on his back.

"He is dead!" Pa wailed and ran to him. "Louie is dead!"

"A stomach pump!" I shouted. "His stomach must be emptied!" I rushed to the phone.

Pa knelt weeping beside Uncle Louie. "Speak to me, my beloved brother," Pa beseeched him. "Speak to me, companion of my youth. Speak!"

Uncle Louie stared in anguish at the ceiling.

I got Doctor Samyotis, who had a little office on the boulevard about a block away, and he promised to come at once. I rushed over to where Pa cradled Uncle Louie's head just in time to hear a terrible rattle rise out of Uncle Louie's throat.

"His death cry!" Pa shouted. "Get a priest!"

"Take it easy, Pa," I said. "The doctor will be here in a minute."

"Too late," Pa wailed. "My brother will be gone."

"Don't give up hope, Pa," I said. I opened Uncle Louie's collar. He sure looked awful.

The door banged open, and Doctor Samyotis came in He took one look at Uncle Louie. "In the kitchen," he snapped. "Carry him back there."

Pa and I picked up Uncle Louie and carried him into the kitchen.

"Put him on the table," Doctor Samyotis said. "Get a pail. The ambulance is coming."

We set him down, and I felt a little sick myself. I left Pa to help the doctor and walked back to the front. A truck driver had come in and was nonchalantly sitting at the counter.

"We are closed," I said.

"I just want a bowl of soup," he said.

"We are closed," I said. "Get out."

"Whadyumean closed?" he said. "I just want a bowl of soup."

From the kitchen Uncle Louie wailed a terrible cry of anguish and doom.

The guy made it to the door in a single leap. I locked up and sat down to wait. I was worn out.

In a few moments the ambulance pulled up in front of the store. I unlocked the door, and two white-coated guys came in with a collapsible stretcher. I waved them into the kitchen.

In another few moments they came out carrying Uncle Louie. He was covered with a blanket to his throat, and a towel was wrapped around his head. All that showed was his mouth, and poor Uncle Louie wasn't smiling.

Pa came out with Doctor Samyotis.

"Doc," I asked, "will Uncle Louie be all right?"

"He will be all right," Doctor Samyotis said. "Just sick for a while."

The attendants loaded Uncle Louie in the ambulance. A small crowd of railroad workers gathered around outside and peered in through the plate-glass window.

Pa started to get his coat. Doctor Samyotis stopped him. "You stay here!" he barked. "Go bury those turkeys!"

Pa stared shamefaced at the floor.

The doctor walked out and slammed the door. The ambulance pulled away.

A FEW GUYS still stared through the window. Pa made a fierce face through the glass, and they scattered. He came back and sat despondently at one of the tables.

"What have I done?" Pa said, and he rocked back and forth like a mourner. "What have I done?"

"It wasn't entirely your fault, Pa," I said.

He shook his head somberly. "He might have died," he said. "Poor Louie might have died."

"It would have been worse if it was a customer," I said. "We might have gotten sued."

"Shut up!" Pa said. "You have no family feeling."

I didn't say anything more because I knew how stricken he was about Uncle Louie.

At that moment the front door opened and Sam Anastis

came in as if he had sprung out of the earth. He stood beaming his hot wide smile at us. I was afraid to look at Pa.

"Greetings," Sam Anastis glowed. "I was passing by and thought I would stop and inquire how went the turkeys? Are they roasted yet?"

I finally looked at Pa, and his face was impassive, but there was a blue vein swelling in his forehead and his cheeks were gathering red with blood.

"Welcome, Sam Anastis," Pa said in a strangely gentle voice. "What a friend you were to bring those turkeys to me."

"What did I tell you?" Sam Anastis trumpeted. "I made nothing on that sale, but for friends like you I don't care."

He saw Pa approaching. For a moment a cloud of uneasiness swept his face. Then it was too late. Pa reached him, and I held my breath. But Pa just clapped him softly on the shoulder.

Seeing Pa close enough to feel the heat shaking off his cheeks made Sam Anastis realize something was wrong. He tried to smile away his fear, but by that time Pa had his arm and began to walk him back to the kitchen.

"Come and see the turkeys, Sam Anastis," Pa said. "I will make you a little sandwich."

Sam Anastis looked shocked. He had an iron-clad rule against eating anything he sold. "I have just eaten," he laughed weakly. "I am not a bit hungry. I never eat this time of day."

By the time they got to the kitchen door, Sam Anastis was dragging his heels. Pa graciously all but lifted him through the door and turned back to me. "You!" he barked. "Call Doctor Samyotis!"

I went quickly to the phone and dialed the doctor's office. He wasn't back yet, and I left urgent word with the nurse for him to come. For Pa's sake, I hoped he would make it in time.

As I hung up, a terrible cry of lament and despair sounded from the kitchen. I got my coat and hurried out the door. I didn't want to go all through that again. Besides, if I hurried, I might still get a bet down in the last race at Jamaica.

THE EYES OF LOVE

AUTUMN came and passed quickly that year. Almost overnight the last dry, brown leaves burned in the twilight
street fires. The nights began to turn cold, and in my basement flat the steam sputtered and hissed through the
overhead radiators. I pushed my bed away from the window
in the bedroom and pulled a woolen blanket from the
shelf in the closet.

I didn't really mind the winter. I preferred it to the
false faces of spring and summer, the ephemeral masks of
buds and flowers that concealed the desolation underneath.
The season I liked best of all was autumn, when the air
smelled definably of death, and the declining days wore
their proper raiment.

I was a writer of stories and a couple of novels that
had been reviewed well in the *New York Times*. They produced a small spasm of activity in the book-review columns

and a sparse display with my picture in one of the down-town book stores. Then, like the tide coming in across a beach littered with debris, the cut-glass fragments of my fame were once more submerged in anonymity.

But writing was still the only thing I wanted to do, even though I had realized years before how senseless was a writer's dream that he could, within the pages of a book, cultivate a garden beyond the darkness of his death. In addition, the stories provided me a meager living and saved me from forty hours a week in another man's vineyard.

Each day I rose early in the morning and slipped into worn sneakers and old pants. I enjoyed a pot of hot, rous-ing coffee and then wrote at my typewriter till afternoon, when the children broke loose in squealing joy from school.

There was a basement flat similar to my own across the narrow court, and it was occupied by a piano teacher I had never seen. Each day after school her students banged out a shrill and discordant series of scales. To evade their wretched hammering I walked down to the corner tavern and lingered for a couple of hours over beer.

In the twilight I returned to my flat and shaved and dressed in more formal clothes. I ate a steak in a neighbor-hood restaurant and marinated it with a glass or two of red wine. When I sold a story and had a new check in my pocket, I treated myself to a full bottle of good wine. Then, with my normally somber nature submerged beneath the laughter of the grape, I would ardently search out some young lady in a tavern and tempt her to join my celebra-tion. This was a kind of gaiety that could not survive the sober dawn, and in the morning I had a mountain of a head and a tongue like the moss on a rock.

It was on such a night in that autumn, preparing for a small celebration because the check for a sale had been meager, that I passed the piano teacher's flat. Through a partially raised shade I saw that she was a young woman with dark, long hair sitting on a bench before an upright piano.

Later in the evening, after I had consumed a half-bottle of wine, I thought of her again. She had been attractive and young. Each afternoon her talentless students drove me from my rooms, and that seemed a legitimate grievance on which to base a visit. I took along what was left of the bottle of wine.

When I reached her apartment, the shades were all drawn closed. I thought she might be asleep or out and then I saw a shadow of movement along the rim of a shade. I rang her bell.

In a moment the door opened just a few inches and I heard the jangle of a chain.

"I beg your pardon," I said, and couldn't see her face. "I live in the basement flat across the court. I was just passing and felt it was time to introduce myself."

She was silent and wary for a moment. "It's a little late, isn't it?" she asked.

"We are artists," I said amiably. "You a musician and I a writer. We understand that time is the greatest irrelevance of all."

I couldn't be sure in the shadows but it seemed to me she smiled. "I have heard you typing for hours at a time."

"I have heard your students at their lessons," I said. "An unusually talented group."

"I'm sorry if they disturb your work."

"Not at all," I said, "but I would be interested in knowing whether they use hammers on the keys?"

She laughed a pleasant sound that dispersed some of the wariness.

"My name is Pete Zachary," I said, "and perhaps we could visit for a few moments."

She hesitated a moment longer and then made up her mind. She closed the door and drew off the chain and then opened the door again. With a triumphant swagger I stepped inside her apartment.

I followed her into the living room. There was only a small lamp burning on a table in the corner, and most of the room was draped in shadow. The upright piano took up almost one entire wall, and on a couch across from the piano reclined a gray, furry cat that regarded me with ominous yellow eyes.

Off the living room was small kitchen similar to my own with a table and two chairs and an assortment of plates and glasses in an open cabinet. There was a large shelf along the wall decorated with several heads of sculpture, carved and polished heads of men and women, that seemed suspended without bodies on the wall.

"My name is Andrea," she said, "and the cat is Emily." At the sound of her name the cat rose and stretched indolently and then leaped with a sinister warning to the floor.

"Pleased to meet you both," I said and sat down.

Andrea sat down on an ottoman across the room from the lamp so that she was darkly concealed in shadow. From as much as I could discern, she was an attractive girl, slender-bodied with good legs. Her hair framed her face and the skin of her cheeks gleamed pale in the shadows and gave an impression of ghostly beauty. But the most striking thing about her were her hands. They were pale, paler than the hue of her face, and the fingers flowed from her slim wrists as if they were long-petaled flowers.

"What kind of things do you write?"

"Short stories mostly," I said. "A couple of novels that did nothing. My creations disappear into the water like small pebbles or finish on a table of remainders at forty-nine cents apiece."

"Are you a beatnik or an angry young man?" she asked with a trace of humor in her voice.

"I'm not revolting against a thing," I said, and the wine loosened my tongue. "All is vanity and vexation of the spirit. Nothing is worth fighting about." I shook my head. "What about you? What makes a young, attractive girl became a teacher to a bunch of piano butchers?"

"That is the way I make my living," she said, "and they're not all butchers. One or two are even very good."

"Things are tough all over," I said and then realized I was still clutching the half-full bottle of wine. "I was taking some wine home. Would you like a small glass?"

"No, thank you," she said, becoming wary again. "But you have a glass if you like."

I walked toward the cabinet. "This place is laid out exactly like mine," I said. There was a lamp on the cabinet and I switched it on to locate a glass. I poured an extra glass and carried it to her.

"You really should try a sip," I said. "It's good sauterne." She raised her head as I reached her. The lamp I had turned on glowed light across her face. She stood staring at a point just beyond my shoulder, not looking at the glass or me, and I realized that she was blind.

I was fiercely shaken and, as if she understood, she spoke quickly to cover my disorder. "I will try a sip," she said and raised her hand to take the glass from me without a trace of fumbling.

"I'll have a glass myself," I said, "and then I'd better leave. It is late, and I shouldn't really have disturbed you." I drank my wine quickly.

I hesitated a moment and then walked toward the door. She rose from the ottoman and followed me. We stood for an instant by the door. "I am sorry about the students," she said softly. "I'll make sure my windows are closed."

"That's all right," I said quickly. "Don't worry about me. I'm through writing by then anyway."

I opened the door and walked out. She was a dark, slender figure against the light, her face concealed again in shadow.

"Goodnight, Pete," she said in a calm and pleasant voice.

"Goodnight, Andrea," I said. She closed the door quietly.

Instead of returning to the bar, I went home. Coldly sober by that time, I mourned the impulse that had sent me to her door. If the world were full of grief and affliction, there was no need for a man to search it out. I felt sorry for her, but there was nothing I could do. I went to bed.

In the first total snap of darkness as I closed the lamp, I wondered what her life was like, denied the sight of faces, figures, fruits, and flowers, the red of a sunset, and the green of grass. After a while I was grateful when I could make out dim familiar objects in my room. But there was also a strange serenity about her that I found moving in recollection, the loveliness of her pale, slim fingers and the softness of her voice. It took me a long time to fall asleep.

THE RAIN started the following Friday night and kept falling all day Saturday until late afternoon. I wrote for a while and then sat by the window smoking a cigarette, watching the water strike the streets and sweep in swift currents to the sewers.

I was hungry, and there was nothing in the place to eat. I put on a raincoat and an old felt hat and ran to the corner to a Chinese restaurant. I ordered a large carton of chow mein and carried it straight to Andrea's door as if I had meant to do that all along.

She answered the door in slacks and blouse, a thin yellow ribbon holding back her fine, black hair. I had the feeling even before I spoke that she knew it was me.

"Andrea," I said, "I've got enough chow mein for two. You interested?"

She smiled and motioned me in quickly out of the rain. I hesitated. "I'm dripping wet," I said.

"Give me your things," she laughed. "I'll hang them in the bathroom to dry."

While she took my wet things inside, I unlaced my sodden shoes and stepped out of them.

"Bring the chow mein in here," she called from the kitchen. I crossed the room, and on the couch Emily somberly turned her head and looked at me with her baleful yellow eyes.

We carried two plates of chow mein back to the living room.

"If you don't mind sitting on the floor," Andrea said, "we can use the coffee table under the window."

"I always eat better on the floor," I said.

She sat down, folding her legs lithely beneath her. I sat down across from her. The window was a square of gray light, and the rain cracked against the panes of glass.

I watched her as we ate. Now that she was visible in a better light, I saw that she was very lovely. The ribbon held her hair, but a single strand had come loose and hung down across her cheek. Even as I noticed, she raised her hand and swept the fallen lock back into place.

"This is wonderful," she said between swallows. "Much better than the hamburger I was going to fry."

Emily came slowly from the couch to sniff the plates. She rubbed her furry back in silent appeal against Andrea's leg.

"Do you think it would bother her?" Andrea asked.

"She may never drink milk again," I said, "but forever after demand pekoe tea with fortune cookies."

"I'll chance that." Andrea laughed and gave her what was left in her plate.

"I'm sorry about the other night," I said, "busting in here like I did half-tanked."

She smiled slightly and bent her head to conceal the smile. "You were so surprised," she said. "You came in here like a jolly bulldog and left like a remorseful Chihuahua."

"I was full of wine," I said ruefully.

She drew up her legs and clasped her arms around her knees. Her face changed under a pensive and solitary withdrawal.

"People are always much more sensitive about blindness than the blind," she said. "When you are blind you get used to it."

"How long has it been for you?" I asked.

"About twelve years now," she said. "I spent eight of those years in an institute for the blind. I came out four years ago and took some college work back home and then came to Chicago and started giving piano lessons to support myself."

"What do they teach you in an institute?"

She smiled pensively again, and her nose twitched in recollection as if she had bitten on a sour plum. "You learn to find the end of a piece of meat with your fork and cut it off with your knife. You learn about social graces and adjustment to society. You learn to try never to fumble because any fumbling you do will make people pity you and remind them you are blind." She paused and grimaced. "But all that sounds very scientific and orderly. What it comes down to is that you learn what it is to be a donkey in a world of horses."

"The things most people take for granted," I said, "must be the things you have to learn all over again."

"The beginning is the worst," she said and she seemed to be listening to the sound of the rain against the glass. "It happened to me when I was ten years old after meningitis. Emily Dickinson wrote of dying, and years later when I read her poems I understood that is the way it is; as if a fly came with an uncertain, stumbling buzz between the light and you, and then the windows close, and then you cannot see." She shifted her body slightly on the floor. "Do you know Emily Dickinson's poems?"

"Some of them," I said.

"I have all her poems in Braille," she said. "They don't consider her too fashionable anymore, but she does well for me." She stroked the cat, who raised her head and stared ominously at me. "Emily here is named after her." For a moment she did not speak. "Now what about you?" she said. "Have you been writing long?"

"Since the Korean war," I said. "I was going to do a great war novel, better than Shaw and Mailer, but it never worked out. I worked on a newspaper for a while and wrote stories at night. About four years ago I sold my first story and published my first novel about a year later. I've managed to make enough by writing to eat and pay the rent and get drunk every once in a while."

"On wine?" she asked.

"On wine," I said. "It's more genteel than Scotch or gin."

"Don't you have a girl?" she asked.

"I was engaged to a girl right after the war," I said. "She broke it off because her parents felt I was indolent, lazy, and shiftless because I wouldn't take a steady job. She agreed with them, and they were all right."

"Where is she now?"

"Who knows? Married to another poor slob and making

his life as happy as she would probably have made mine."

"You sound so old and weary," she said.

"In this gilded age," I said, "you don't have to grow old to feel weary. Even the young perch on their ash heaps and wait like Job for the next disaster." I paused to light a cigarette. "Where you from?" I asked.

"A little town in Kansas," she said. "My father was a pharmacist there and lived with my mother in a frame house with a long porch that I was born in."

The room had grown darker, and I could barely make out the white fabric of her blouse. The rain grew faint and left only the sound of water gurgling in the gutters.

"How did you happen to come here alone?" I said.

"Whenever my mother kissed me I could feel the tears on her cheeks," she said. "And every time my father walked into my room I could sense his grief and despair. They loved me very much, but they were full of pity and wouldn't let me live. I write them that I am living with three other girls, gay and friendly girls, who take good care of me."

"You've got guts," I said.

"I'm not at all brave," she said with a trace of scorn for herself in her voice. "I'm not always cheerful either. I left home simply because I couldn't bear their pity. There was even a boy who took me to dances, and his nobility rose like wind from his pores, and everybody in town praised him for dating a poor, blind girl."

"You're a good-looking girl," I said. "Maybe you weren't fair to him."

"There have been a few others like him," she said defiantly. "Men intent on a quick moment of pleasure and willing to concede that sometimes a woman has no need of sight. But I don't need that kind of love."

A silence settled between us. The room was completely dark by then. I felt a vague unrest and moved to rise.

"Let me turn on a light," she said. "You'll stumble and fall."

She rose and crossed the dark room swiftly and switched on a lamp. The light hurt my eyes for a moment. She stood there, slender in her slacks and blouse, her face a pale oval within the frame of her hair.

"Will you read me something you've written?" she asked.

"Sure," I said, "but don't expect Emily Dickinson."

She brought me my coat and hat, and we stood a moment by the door.

"You're tall," she said slowly. "You have a strong voice, a little weary sometimes, but with a good tone. What do you really look like?"

"You'd never mistake me for a movie star," I said. "My face is what a pulp writer would call weatherbeaten."

"I can imagine you any way I wish," she said. She smiled and extended her hands toward me. Her fingertips made a soft and subtle contact with my cheeks. I had never known that a woman's hands could be that gentle. They touched my temples and moved across my eyes and slipped down my cheeks. "Your eyes are set in deep hollows," she said, and there was a look of waiting and listening on her face. "I think your nose is too broad. Your upper lip is full, and you have a sharp cleft in your chin and you need a shave."

The touch of her fingers carried a pressing warmth through my body, and I felt an urgent longing to touch her. I bent and kissed her then, first on the forehead, lightly and with gentleness, and then with urgency, hard on her lovely lips. When I reached out to hold her, she pulled away.

"What do you want?" she asked, and a strange hardness had entered her voice. "What do you want?"

"Andrea," I said, "listen . . ."

"Do you love me already?" she said, and there was no mistaking her baleful mockery. "Is it desire you feel without love, or just pity for the poor little blind music teacher?"

"I just wanted to kiss you," I said. "Emily Dickinson would have understood."

A shadow of remorse swept her face, and then she shook it off. "Thanks anyway for the chop suey."

"Chow mein," I said.

"All right," she said and relented slightly with a trace of a smile.

"Some day this next week," I said, "I'll borrow a car and we'll go for a drive."

She was silent for a moment. "Maybe," she said finally. "We'll see."

I HAD never put credence in the myth that love might begin at first sight, by a look or by the touch of a hand. And I had always mocked those sonnets of passion that mediocre poets wrote in flame. But that winter, those days and nights of cold and snow, I woke in the morning without a sense of burden in the beginning of another day. For the first time in years I could endure the twilight becoming darkness without a wavering of my spirit.

Andrea and I took long walks together in the park. We sat closely together on a bench beneath the black trunk of a cold, bare tree. When she listened raptly to the scurrying of a squirrel, or ran her hands along the hard, frozen bark of a tree, or felt a change in the wind I could not hear, it was as if we were both young again, on an earth that still retained its magic. When I was with her it was strangely true that all things recaptured their edges, became sharp for me where they had been blurred.

"Andrea, do you believe in God?" I asked her one day in the park.

"Yes," she said quietly.

"Blindness has not made you bitter?"

"If I had not become blind," she answered softly, "I might have lived my years taking the earth for granted. My blindness has made me search again to discover all things anew. Is not God somewhere in this search?"

There were the evenings in her flat when I lay on the couch while she played a melancholy sonata or a gay song that echoed the wild whirling of figures in a lovers' dance. We ate and drank together, and the stain of wine glistened upon her lips, and it was true that she came upon the desert of my days as if she were a flower.

But there was always a wariness in the hours we spent together, an evident fear in her at what was growing between us. When I tried to kiss her she drew back in guarded restraint, so that I grew apprehensive, too, and all that winter did not speak of the way I felt. Until one night, one night when I could not contain myself any longer, I broke the silence that held us apart.

She had moved from the bench of the piano and had come over to where I lay on the couch. She sat on the floor with her head near my knees, and the moon fell across her face, a white and glistening vision. I touched her hair, felt the fine strands tingle beneath my palms, and understood how aware she had made me of touch. The thought of having her as my wife suddenly possessed me with a wild sweetness such as I had never known.

"I love you, Andrea," I said.

She withdrew her head from near my knees. Her open fingers which had been lying on the cloth near my hands flew back to her lap.

"There is an old folk legend," I said, "that speaks of a blind man joined with one who is lame. They journey together until they find the healing waters and are both restored."

"I don't want to talk of love," she said. She rose from the floor and went to stand beside the window.

"Are you going to spend the rest of your life alone?" I asked. "In this little flat, in these dark rooms, teaching piano to unhappy children?"

"I can look after myself," she said. "I don't need anyone to look after me."

"We all need somebody," I said.

"I can look after myself," she said, and the words came ripped from her flesh. "I don't need pity."

She moved away from the window, away from me, into the darkness at the other end of the room. She sealed herself against me, retreated into silence that she wore as if it were armor. And I was left alone in the beam of the futile and bright moon that seemed to be hanging just above the roof of the building across the street.

I DID not see Andrea for several weeks after that night. I wrote hard, harder than I had in years, and drank much more, and spent a good deal of time walking alone in the desolate park. I felt her everywhere, and yet pride and anger kept me from her door. In the afternoon, when the children played their scales at her piano, it filled me with a fierce melancholia. Sometimes walking past her flat at night I paused in the darkness and waited for a quick, furtive glimpse of her within the basement rooms.

The first traces of spring appeared in the city. Great

winds swept the streets at night, and in the parks and gardens the earth stirred and waited. I listened to the wind shake the panes of my windows and knew Andrea must have been listening to the wild wind as well. In the morning the sun felt a shade warmer. Then, one day in early April, a sparrow perched on my sill and in the quick flutter of its jubilant step I knew the spring had come.

Near the end of April on an afternoon, while leaving my flat to go for a beer, I passed a small moving truck parked outside in the street. As it pulled away I noticed an upright piano secured with rope and cloth. Under a sudden apprehension, I looked at Andrea's windows, and the shades were up and the curtains were gone. I went down the stairs and tried the door. When it opened I walked inside. I called her name, and there was no answer. The furniture was gone, and the rooms were empty. I turned in despair to leave, thinking of ways to pursue the truck, when a small, furry body moved beside the stove in the kitchen and caught my eye. Emily came slowly over to look at me, and I knew that Andrea would be back.

I waited until twilight fell. The street lights went on and threw sharp beams of light through the uncurtained windows across the bare wood floor. I found some milk in the icebox and poured a saucer for Emily, but she rejected my offering.

It must have been some time later when I heard the car outside. I looked out the window and saw the taxi from which Andrea had emerged. A moment later she entered the apartment. I made no sound, and yet she knew at once I was there.

"Pete," she said, and I couldn't understand whether there was sorrow or gladness in her voice.

"You were running away," I said bitterly. "You were going to leave and say nothing to me."

She made a helpless motion with her hands.

"Then go, damn you," I said. "I understand you now. When you say you don't want pity it is really pity that you want. You want to remain alone because then people will always pity you."

"You have no right," she said, and her voice was a thin, tight whisper, "no right to say that to me."

"Emily has more courage than you," I said savagely. "She at least goes prowling in the midnight alleys and comes back in the dawn with her fur ruffled and shreds of skin under her claws. But you are afraid of love."

She twisted her body as if to flee, and then something made her turn back, and the sight of her cold white cheeks swept the anger from my body.

"When I found you my life was nothing," I said. "You taught me a new way of seeing a tree and a flower. A new way of understanding the earth and hearing the wind. You taught me that all life is connected by the touch of a hand. Don't take that from me now."

For a long moment she did not move. She seemed to be holding her breath. Then she walked slowly to where I stood and raised her face to mine and lifted her hands to my cheeks. Her breath came out in a long shaken sigh. She did not speak, but for the first time touched me in a fierce caress. She touched my eyes and touched my lips and her hands trembled with love. And for the first time since I was a child, I cried again for the great wonder and beauty of life.

THE RETURN OF KATERINA

In April of that year, Paul Brademas had been dead two years. His widow, Katerina, lived with his father, Lycurgus, in a small apartment above their tavern.

After his son's death, Lycurgus wished to sell the tavern. He was almost sixty himself and wearied of the long hours on his feet. In addition he did not think it proper that a young attractive woman such as Katerina should work in the smoky room of boisterous men.

But Katerina insisted they keep the tavern which brought in a good profit. When she worked hard there was little time left to brood upon the death of her husband. She also felt it provided Lycurgus a meeting place for a few old friends with whom he could sit in the evening.

In the beginning Katerina's grief for her husband was a wild despair. For a while the memory of their lovemaking was something she could recall at will. At those times she felt her breath become short and her breasts grow taut.

And so strong was the love she held for him that she could almost feel again his hands across her body and the strength of his arms about her waist.

But time passed and the seasons changed. In the winter the snow piled in drifts before the tavern. Katerina would rise early to clean the walk before the old man rose. When he came downstairs he would grumble that shoveling was man's work and take the shovel from her hands.

In the spring of the second year after her husband's death, a strange restlessness possessed Katerina. She was no longer satisfied to recall her husband in dreams. She walked in the glittering twilight and felt envy growing in her heart at the sight of lovers in the park.

She visited her husband's grave and placed fresh flowers upon the mound of earth. In those moments under the sighing trees she wept and swore eternal love. She waited for some sign that he had heard and understood but the earth made no gesture of redemption.

In the evenings in the tavern she no longer took pleasure in the wild laughter of the men. She became snappish and cross. Her temper flared quickly and she acquired a reputation for an acid tongue. Lycurgus was concerned for her and tried to ease her labor in different ways thinking that perhaps she was working too hard.

After closing he sent her to bed at once and swept the floor himself and locked the door. The only person left inside was his old friend, Zakinthákis, veteran of ten thousand drinking bouts and three wars. A wise rascal of a man who counted his life of fighting and wenching well spent. Lycurgus disapproved of his friend's morals but enjoyed his company.

After counting the cash Lycurgus took a final glass of mastiha to the table for himself and another for Zakinthákis. They toasted each other solemnly.

"I am troubled over Katerina," the old man told Zakinthákis. "Nothing seems to please her. She has grown as peevish as an old woman."

Zakinthákis looked into his glass of mastiha and a faint zestful smile curled his thin lips. He admired the fine lush body of Katerina and knew the reason for her distemper. He wished he could still have been the one to comfort her.

"When Paul was alive," Lycurgus said sadly, "she was not like that. They loved each other dearly." He wiped a stray tear from his eye. "It must be her grief," he said. "She still mourns for him."

Zakinthákis sipped at his mastiha and marveled at how a man could have lived as many years as Lycurgus and still understand so little about women.

"Grief is a terrible thing," he said somberly, and within him he laughed because he knew that when he died a thousand women would grieve for him . . . but not for long. Then because the long evening of drinking had dulled him slightly, he spoke without thinking. "She needs a lover," he said.

Lycurgus sat shocked and rooted to his chair. His lips moved and no words came. Then he found his voice and let out an angry roar.

"Devil!" he shouted. "Lecher and animal out of darkness! Have you lost your mind?"

Zakinthákis realized his mistake and sighed. He rose heavily to his feet to leave. Lycurgus followed him raging to the door.

"You dare speak of my son's wife in that way!" he cried. "Get out, you stepson of some unholy devil!"

Long after Zakinthákis had left, Lycurgus still paced the tavern and hurled curses upon his friend's head. Each time he considered the outrage, his blood flamed anew.

Finally he turned off the last lights and went upstairs.

Outside the bedroom of Katerina he listened for a moment at her door. There was no sound from her room and he went to bed.

For a long time he could not sleep. The murmur of the night came through his window. He was restlessly aware of his age and his inevitable death. The years had swept by so quickly. He had never traveled, never cared for cards or drink, and had been shy with girls. A day came when he married because he could not bear his loneliness any longer. His wife had been a dark and thin woman who wore black for mourning all her life. Rarely would she suffer Lycurgus to caress her and from one of these uncertain, unsatisfying unions their only child had been born. But the child was little comfort to Lycurgus because of the domination of the mother. In the boy's seventeenth year, his mother died, accepting death as gratefully as a suppliant. Lycurgus could not grieve for her and accepted joyously the return of his son. When Paul married Katerina he wept for their happiness and for his own good fortune. He envisioned the day that grandchildren would scamper around him. But then the young man had fallen sick, and after a short shocking illness had died. As if his mother, dark and brooding from the grave, had called to him to join her.

Lycurgus tossed in helpless despair. Then he remembered Katerina in the room beside his own. Her nearness was a comfort to him, and he slept.

SPRING passed into summer. The heat came early in the day and twilight brought no relief. Along the street on which they lived men and women sat before the stores, fanning themselves until long past midnight. The boys and girls ran by squealing to slap one another's bottoms in the dark alleys.

After closing the tavern Lycurgus and Katerina walked for a while in the park. On the grass in long uneven rows, men, women and children slept under the sky. A great sound of whispering, like the drone of countless crickets, rose from the dark and hidden groves.

Back in their flat with the open windows providing no relief from the heat, Lycurgus lay awake in the dark listening to Katerina in her room. He heard her talking to herself, and though he could not make out the words he heard the bitterness in her voice. Once he thought he heard her weeping, and because he felt she wept for her dead, he cried with her, silently, so she would not hear.

ON A NIGHT in August a group of strangers came to the tavern. They were loud and bold young men, blond Norsemen, and they drank great quantities of beer. Countless times during the evening Katerina carried trays of beer to their table. They laughed and teased her and a bright flush of pink appeared in her cheeks. They finally left, holding one another up, and the bawdy sound of their voices could be heard rioting from the street.

The next night one of them, a blond young giant with big hands, returned alone. He sat in a corner and did not sing or carry on. Katerina served him several times and lingered at his table.

From that night on the blond stranger came every evening. Whenever he could, Lycurgus served the man whose light pale eyes seemed full of menace. Lycurgus was reminded of tales he had heard as a child of the villages raided by the pillaging Turks. The burning of houses and the screaming of women.

An evening came when several hours before closing, Katerina told him she was not well. He suggested she go at once to bed but she wished to walk alone for a while and he let her go. It was not until she had left that he noticed for the first time in several weeks that the blond stranger was not at his table in the corner. A cold fear enveloped him but he remembered Katerina's sacred allegiance to her dead and suppressed his apprehension.

SUMMER passed and the first winds of autumn swept the scent of burning leaves along the street. The days grew shorter and there was a strange still beauty in the crisp nights.

With the passing of summer, Katerina took on a new grace. Lycurgus marveled at the change. She had thrown off the terrible melancholia and once again enjoyed the laughter in the tavern. Her black hair gleamed lustrous and alive and her body once more appeared lithe and supple. He heard her sing in her room at night.

In the morning as she cooked him breakfast, he basked in her radiance and marveled at how beautiful she had become once again. He watched her eat with pleasure, the ripe soft lips parting slightly and the small pieces of food going between them. Her cheeks were as soft and unblemished as those of a child and the color of her flesh was the cool, transparent whiteness of the foam on new milk.

When they had finished she rose from the table and carried the dishes to the sink. She spoke softly with her back to him.

"Papa, I am going away," she said. "I am going to the country for a little while. Now when the leaves are changing and the earth is so beautiful."

"Going away?" Lycurgus said in alarm. "Katerina, you cannot go away alone!"

"For just a little while," she said gently. "I am weary suddenly of the city and the noise and the disorder."

"It is not right that you go alone," Lycurgus said. "We

will close the tavern. We will go away together so that I can look after you."

"I wish to go alone," she said, and then she added quickly, "You do not like to travel. You would come only because you are concerned for me." She bent over the dishes in the sink. "Zakinthákis can help you in the tavern. I will be gone only a little while."

"Zakinthákis!" the old man cried. "I would sooner ask help of the devil!"

"Then find someone else to help you," she said and there was a firmness in her voice.

She left the following Friday and was gone for almost two weeks. Lycurgus missed her terribly. At night he could not bear to go to their rooms and stayed downstairs in the tavern long after closing. In loneliness and desperation he accepted the return of Zakinthákis and drank with him for hours.

"She could have waited until I died," he complained bitterly to his friend. "She could have taken her vacation then."

Zakinthákis merely sighed.

At the end of the second week Katerina returned. On a night after Lycurgus had closed the tavern and sat drinking with Zakinthákis.

He had turned off most of the lights and when he heard the door he thought he had forgotten to lock it and that some patron had entered. Then he heard her voice speak his name and a great gladness leaped in his heart. He rose quickly from the table.

"Katerina!" he cried. "Katerina!"

It was not until then that he saw she was not alone. Only when his eyes became accustomed to the shadows about the door, did he recognize the tall blond stranger.

A terrible distress ran riot in his body. He wanted to cry out but no sound passed his lips. He stared at the silent figure beside Katerina. Never had he hated a man more. He would not let himself think but only let the hot flow of hate sweep over him in waves.

"Papa," Katerina said, and her cheeks gleamed pale in the shadows. "This is my husband, Edwin Larsen."

Then Lycurgus cried out. A cry of pain and anguish. A cry for his dead son and for deceit and the fiendish heart of a woman. He burned suddenly under a white hot flame.

"Thief!" he said to Edwin Larsen, and smoke and fury curled off his tongue. "Vandal, bastard out of darkness!" His voice rose. "I should have killed you the first night I saw you!"

"Papa, try to understand," Katerina said. "I loved Paul very much. You know I loved him." Her voice rose and broke. "But you cannot love the dead forever."

"Not forever!" Lycurgus said and he spoke to her in angry bitterness. "Only two years and you forsake his memory."

"I loved him," Katerina said. "When he died I could have died with him. But I lived and in the summer I saw the new buds spring to life on the trees and heard the lovers whispering in the dark groves."

"Silence!" Lycurgus cried. "I do not wish to hear your shame!"

Katerina turned and reached back for her husband and brought him into the light. "Papa," she said, "Papa, do you want me back? Tell me now. If you want me back I will come back."

Lycurgus looked from her to the stranger. "Alone," he said. "I want you back alone."

"I cannot come alone," she said. "I am married now."

"You are married to my son."

"He is dead," Katerina said.

"I do not want you then!" Lycurgus cried. "I do not want you then!"

Through a mist of grief he saw her turn. Slim beside the tall Norseman, she walked to the door. Her steps made a slight fading sound as she reached the street.

When he could hear her no longer he turned fiercely on Zakinthákis. "Get out," he said. "Leave me alone."

Zakinthákis moved slowly to the door. He paused with his hand on the knob. "I am going," he said. "I will tell you something first, old friend."

"Leave me alone!" Lycurgus cried.

"You do not weep for your son," Zakinthákis said, and his voice was filled with pity and sadness. "You weep for yourself."

And in that instant after the door closed and he was left alone, in that moment of dark revelation, he heard his voice cry her name in the silence. "Katerina!" and only the raven-winged vision of his wife heard and returned to comfort him.

THE WOOING
OF ARIADNE

I KNEW from the beginning she must accept my love—put aside foolish female protestations. It is the distinction of the male to be the aggressor and the cloak of the female to lend grace to the pursuit. Aha! I am wise to these wiles.

I first saw Ariadne at a dance given by the Spartan brotherhood in the Legion Hall on Laramie Street. The usual assemblage of prune-faced and banana-bodied women smelling of virtuous anemia. They were an outrage to a man such as myself.

Then I saw her! A tall stately woman, perhaps in her early thirties. She had firm and slender arms bare to the shoulders and a graceful neck. Her hair was black and thick and piled in a great bun at the back of her head. That grand abundance of hair attracted me at once. This modern aberration women have of chopping their hair close to the scalp and leaving it in fantastic disarray I find revolting.

I went at once to my friend Vasili, the baker, and asked him who she was.

"Ariadne Langos," he said. "Her father is Janco Langos, the grocer."

"Is she engaged or married?"

"No," he said slyly. "They say she frightens off the young men. They say she is very spirited."

"Excellent," I said and marveled at my good fortune in finding her unpledged. "Introduce me at once."

"Marko," Vasili said with some apprehension. "Do not commit anything rash."

I pushed the little man forward. "Do not worry, little friend," I said. "I am a man suddenly possessed by a vision. I must meet her at once."

We walked together across the dance floor to where my beloved stood. The closer we came the more impressive was the majestic swell of her breasts and the fine great sweep of her thighs. She towered over the insignificant apple-core women around her. Her eyes, dark and thoughtful, seemed to be restlessly searching the room.

Be patient, my dove! Marko is coming.

"Miss Ariadne," Vasili said. "This is Mr. Marko Palamas. He desires to have the honor of your acquaintance."

She looked at me for a long and piercing moment. I imagined her gauging my mighty strength by the width of my shoulders and the circumference of my arms. I felt the tips of my mustache bristle with pleasure. Finally she nodded with the barest minimum of courtesy. I was not discouraged.

"Miss Ariadne," I said, "may I have the pleasure of this dance?"

She stared at me again with her fiery eyes. I could imagine more timid men shriveling before her fierce gaze. My heart flamed at the passion her rigid exterior concealed.

"I think not," she said.

"Don't you dance?"

Vasili gasped beside me. An old prune-face standing nearby clucked her toothless gums.

"Yes, I dance," Ariadne said coolly. "I do not wish to dance with you."

"Why?" I asked courteously.

"I do not think you heard me," she said. "I do not wish to dance with you."

Oh, the sly and lovely darling. Her subterfuge so apparent. Trying to conceal her pleasure at my interest.

"Why?" I asked again.

"I am not sure," she said. "It could be your appearance, which bears considerable resemblance to a gorilla, or your manner, which would suggest closer alliance to a pig."

"Now that you have met my family," I said engagingly, "let us dance."

"Not now," she said, and her voice rose. "Not this dance or the one after. Not tonight or tomorrow night or next month or next year. Is that clear?"

Sweet, sweet Ariadne. Ancient and eternal game of retreat and pursuit. My pulse beat more quickly.

Vasili pulled at my sleeve. He was my friend, but without the courage of a goat. I shook him off and spoke to Ariadne.

"There is a joy like fire that consumes a man's heart when he first sets eyes on his beloved," I said. "This I felt when I first saw you." My voice trembled under a mighty passion. "I swear before God from this moment that I love you."

She stared shocked out of her deep dark eyes and, beside her, old prune-face staggered as if she had been kicked. Then my beloved did something which proved indisputably that her passion was as intense as mine.

She doubled up her fist and struck me in the eye. A stout

blow for a woman that brought a haze to my vision, but I shook my head and moved a step closer.

"I would not care," I said, "if you struck out both my eyes. I would cherish the memory of your beauty forever."

By this time the music had stopped, and the dancers formed a circle of idiot faces about us. I paid them no attention and ignored Vasili, who kept whining and pulling at my sleeve.

"You are crazy!" she said. "You must be mad! Remove yourself from my presence or I will tear out both your eyes and your tongue besides!"

You see! Another woman would have cried, or been frightened into silence. But my Ariadne, worthy and venerable, hurled her spirit into my teeth.

"I would like to call on your father tomorrow," I said. From the assembled dancers who watched there rose a few vagrant whispers and some rude laughter. I stared at them carefully and they hushed at once. My temper and strength of arm were well known.

Ariadne did not speak again, but in a magnificent spirit stamped from the floor. The music began, and men and women began again to dance. I permitted Vasili to pull me to a corner.

"You are insane!" he said. He wrung his withered fingers in anguish. "You assaulted her like a Turk! Her relatives will cut out your heart!"

"My intentions were honorable," I said. "I saw her and loved her and told her so." At this point I struck my fist against my chest. Poor Vasili jumped.

"But you do not court a woman that way," he said.

"*You* don't, my anemic-friend," I said. "Nor do the rest of these sheep. But I court a woman that way!"

He looked to heaven and helplessly shook his head. I waved good-by and started for my hat and coat.

"Where are you going?" he asked.

"To prepare for tomorrow," I said. "In the morning I will speak to her father."

I left the hall and in the street felt the night wind cold on my flushed cheeks. My blood was inflamed. The memory of her loveliness fed fuel to the fire. For the first time I understood with a terrible clarity the driven heroes of the past performing mighty deeds in love. Paris stealing Helen in passion, and Menelaus pursuing with a great fleet. In that moment if I knew the whole world would be plunged into conflict I would have followed Ariadne to Hades.

I went to my rooms above my tavern. I could not sleep. All night I tossed in restless frenzy. I touched my eye that she had struck with her spirited hand.

Ariadne! Ariadne! my soul cried out.

In the morning I bathed and dressed carefully. I confirmed the address of Langos, the grocer, and started to his store. It was a bright cold November morning, but I walked with spring in my step.

WHEN I opened the door of the Langos grocery, a tiny bell rang shrilly. I stepped into the store piled with fruits and vegetables and smelling of cabbages and greens.

A stooped little old man with white bushy hair and owlish eyes came toward me. He looked as if his veins contained vegetable juice instead of blood, and if he were, in truth, the father of my beloved I marveled at how he could have produced such a paragon of women.

"Are you Mr. Langos?"

"I am," he said and he came closer. "I am."

"I met your daughter last night," I said. "Did she mention I was going to call?"

He shook his head somberly.

"My daughter mentioned you," he said. "In thirty years

I have never seen her in such a state of agitation. She was possessed."

"The effect on me was the same," I said. "We met for the first time last night, and I fell passionately in love."

"Incredible," the old man said.

"You wish to know something about me," I said. "My name is Marko Palamas. I am a Spartan emigrated to this country eleven years ago. I am forty-one years old. I have been a wrestler and a sailor and fought with the resistance movement in Greece in the war. For this service I was decorated by the king. I own a small but profitable tavern on Dart Street. I attend church regularly. I love your daughter."

As I finished he stepped back and bumped a rack of fruit. An orange rolled off to the floor. I bent and retrieved it to hand it to him, and he cringed as if he thought I might bounce it off his old head.

"She is a bad-tempered girl," he said. "Stubborn, impatient and spoiled. She has been the cause of considerable concern to me. All the eligible young men have been driven away by her temper and disposition."

"Poor girl," I said. "Subjected to the courting of calves and goats."

The old man blinked his owlish eyes. The front door opened and a battleship of a woman sailed in.

"Three pounds of tomatoes, Mr. Langos," she said. "I am in a hurry. Please to give me good ones. Last week two spoiled before I had a chance to put them into Demetri's salad."

"I am very sorry," Mr. Langos said. He turned to me. "Excuse me, Mr. Poulmas."

"Palamas," I said. "Marko Palamas."

He nodded nervously. He went to wait on the battleship, and I spent a moment examining the store. Neat and small. I would not imagine he did more than hold his own. In the rear of the store there were stairs leading to what appeared to be an apartment above. My heart beat faster.

When he had bagged the tomatoes and given change, he returned to me and said, "She is also a terrible cook. She cannot fry an egg without burning it." His voice shook with woe. "She cannot make pilaf or lamb with squash." He paused. "You like pilaf and lamb with squash?"

"Certainly."

"You see?" he said in triumph. "She is useless in the kitchen. She is thirty years old, and I am resigned she will remain an old maid. In a way I am glad because I know she would drive some poor man to drink."

"Do not deride her to discourage me," I said. "You need have no fear that I will mistreat her or cause her unhappiness. When she is married to me she will cease being a problem to you." I paused. "It is true that I am not pretty by the foppish standards that prevail today. But I am a man. I wrestled Zahundos and pinned him two straight falls in Baltimore. A giant of a man. Afterward he conceded he had met his master. This from Zahundos was a mighty compliment."

"I am sure," the old man said without enthusiasm. "I am sure."

He looked toward the front door as if hoping for another customer.

"Is your daughter upstairs?"

He looked startled and tugged at his apron. "Yes," he said. "I don't know. Maybe she has gone out."

"May I speak to her? Would you kindly tell her I wish to speak with her."

"You are making a mistake," the old man said. "A terrible mistake."

"No mistake," I said firmly.

The old man shuffled toward the stairs. He climbed

them slowly. At the top he paused and turned the knob of the door. He rattled it again.

"It is locked," he called down. "It has never been locked before. She has locked the door."

"Knock," I said. "Knock to let her know I am here."

"I think she knows," the old man said. "I think she knows."

He knocked gently.

"Knock harder," I suggested. "Perhaps she does not hear."

"I think she hears," the old man said. "I think she hears."

"Knock again," I said. "Shall I come up and knock for you?"

"No, no," the old man said quickly. He gave the door a sound kick. Then he groaned as if he might have hurt his foot.

"She does not answer," he said in a quavering voice. "I am very sorry she does not answer."

"The coy darling," I said and laughed. "If that is her game." I started for the front door of the store.

I went out and stood on the sidewalk before the store. Above the grocery were the front windows of their apartment. I cupped my hands about my mouth.

"Ariadne!" I shouted. "Ariadne!"

The old man came out the door running disjointedly. He looked frantically down the street.

"Are you mad?" he asked shrilly. "You will cause a riot. The police will come. You must be mad!"

"Ariadne!" I shouted. "Beloved!"

A window slammed open, and the face of Ariadne appeared above me. Her dark hair tumbled about her ears.

"Go away!" she shrieked. "Will you go away!"

"Ariadne," I said loudly. "I have come as I promised. I have spoken to your father. I wish to call on you."

"Go away!" she shrieked. "Madman! Imbecile! Go away!"

By this time a small group of people had assembled around the store and were watching curiously. The old man stood wringing his hands and uttering what sounded like small groans.

"Ariadne," I said. "I wish to call on you. Stop this non-sense and let me in."

She pushed farther out the window and showed me her teeth.

"Be careful, beloved," I said. "You might fall."

She drew her head in quickly, and I turned then to the assembled crowd.

"A misunderstanding," I said. "Please move on."

Suddenly old Mr. Langos shrieked. A moment later something broke on the sidewalk a foot from where I stood. A vase or a plate. I looked up, and Ariadne was preparing to hurl what appeared to be a water pitcher.

"Ariadne!" I shouted. "Stop that!"

The water pitcher landed closer than the vase, and frag-ments of glass struck my shoes. The crowd scattered, and the old man raised his hands and wailed to heaven.

Ariadne slammed down the window.

The crowd moved in again a little closer, and somewhere among them I heard laughter. I fixed them with a cold stare and waited for some one of them to say something offensive. I would have tossed him around like sardines, but they slowly dispersed and moved on. In another mo-ment the old man and I were alone.

I followed him into the store. He walked an awkward dance of agitation. He shut the door and peered out through the glass.

"A disgrace," he wailed. "A disgrace. The whole street will know by nightfall. A disgrace."

"A girl of heroic spirit," I said. "Will you speak to her for me? Assure her of the sincerity of my feelings. Tell her I pledge eternal love and devotion."

The old man sat down on an orange crate and weakly made his cross.

"I had hoped to see her myself," I said. "But if you promise to speak to her, I will return this evening."

"That soon?" the old man said.

"If I stayed now," I said, "it would be sooner."

"This evening," the old man said and shook his head in resignation. "This evening."

I went to my tavern for a while and set up the glasses for the evening trade. I made arrangements for Pavlakis to tend bar in my place. Afterward I sat alone in my apartment and read a little of majestic Pindar to ease the agitation of my heart.

Once in the mountains of Greece when I fought with the guerrillas in the last year of the great war, I suffered a wound from which it seemed I would die. For days high fever raged in my body. My friends brought a priest at night secretly from one of the captive villages to read the last rites. I accepted the coming of death and was grateful for many things. For the gentleness and wisdom of my old grandfather, the loyalty of my companions in war, the years I sailed between the wild ports of the seven seas, and the strength that flowed to me from the Spartan earth. For one thing only did I weep when it seemed I would leave life, that I had never set ablaze the world with a burning song of passion for one woman. Women I had known, pockets of pleasure that I tumbled for quick joy, but I had been denied mighty love for one woman. For that I wept.

In Ariadne I swore before God I had found my woman.

I knew by the storm-lashed hurricane that swept within my body. A woman whose majesty was in harmony with the earth, who would be faithful and beloved to me as Penelope had been to Ulysses.

That evening near seven I returned to the grocery. Deep twilight had fallen across the street, and the lights in the window of the store had been dimmed. The apples and oranges and pears had been covered with brown paper for the night.

I tried the door and found it locked. I knocked on the glass, and a moment later the old man came shuffling out of the shadows and let me in.

"Good evening, Mr. Langos."

He muttered some greeting in answer. "Ariadne is not here," he said. "She is at the church. Father Marlas wishes to speak with you."

"A fine young priest," I said. "Let us go at once."

I waited on the sidewalk while the old man locked the store. We started the short walk to the church.

"A clear and ringing night," I said. "Does it not make you feel the wonder and glory of being alive?"

The old man uttered what sounded like a groan, but a truck passed on the street at that moment and I could not be sure.

At the church we entered by a side door leading to the office of Father Marlas. I knocked on the door, and when he called to us to enter we walked in.

Young Father Marlas was sitting at his desk in his black cassock and with his black goatee trim and imposing beneath his clean-shaven cheeks. Beside the desk, in a dark blue dress sat Ariadne, looking somber and beautiful. A bald-headed, big-nosed old man with flint and fire in his eyes sat in a chair beside her.

"Good evening, Marko," Father Marlas said and smiled.

"Good evening, Father," I said.

"Mr. Langos and his daughter you have met," he said and he cleared his throat. "This is Uncle Paul Langos."

"Good evening, Uncle Paul," I said. He glared at me and did not answer. I smiled warmly at Ariadne in greeting, but she was watching the priest.

"Sit down," Father Marlas said.

I sat down across from Ariadne, and old Mr. Langos took a chair beside Uncle Paul. In this way we were arrayed in battle order as if we were opposing armies.

A long silence prevailed during which Father Marlas cleared his throat several times. I observed Ariadne closely. There were grace and poise even in the way her slim-fingered hands rested in her lap. She was a dark and lovely flower, and my pulse beat more quickly at her nearness.

"Marko," Father Marlas said finally. "Marko, I have known you well for the three years since I assumed duties in this parish. You are most regular in your devotions and very generous at the time of the Christmas and Easter offerings. Therefore, I find it hard to believe this complaint against you."

"My family are not liars!" Uncle Paul said, and he had a voice like hunks of dry hard cheese being grated.

"Of course not," Father Marlas said quickly. He smiled benevolently at Ariadne. "I only mean to say—"

"Tell him to stay away from my niece," Uncle Paul burst out.

"Excuse me, Uncle Paul," I said very politely. "Will you kindly keep out of what is not your business."

Uncle Paul looked shocked. "Not my business?" He looked from Ariadne to Father Marlas and then to his brother. "Not my business?"

"This matter concerns Ariadne and me," I said. "With outside interference it becomes more difficult."

"Not my business!" Uncle Paul said. He couldn't seem to get that through his head.

"Marko," Father Marlas said, and his composure was slightly shaken. "The family feels you are forcing your attention upon this girl. They are concerned."

"I understand, Father," I said. "It is natural for them to be concerned. I respect their concern. It is also natural for me to speak of love to a woman I have chosen for my wife."

"Not my business!" Uncle Paul said again, and shook his head violently.

"My daughter does not wish to become your wife," Mr. Langos said in a squeaky voice.

"That is for your daughter to say," I said courteously.

ARIADNE made a sound in her throat, and we all looked at her. Her eyes were deep and cold, and she spoke slowly and carefully as if weighing each word on a scale in her father's grocery.

"I would not marry this madman if he were one of the Twelve Apostles," she said.

"See!" Mr. Langos said in triumph.

"Not my business!" Uncle Paul snarled.

"Marko," Father Marlas said. "Try to understand."

"We will call the police!" Uncle Paul raised his voice. "Put this hoodlum under a bond!"

"Please!" Father Marlas said. "Please!"

"Today he stood on the street outside the store," Mr. Langos said excitedly. "He made me a laughingstock."

"If I were a younger man," Uncle Paul growled, "I would settle this without the police. Zi-ip!" He drew a callused finger violently across his throat.

"Please," Father Marlas said.

"A disgrace!" Mr. Langos said.

"An outrage!" Uncle Paul said.

"He must leave Ariadne alone!" Mr. Langos said.

"We will call the police!" Uncle Paul said.

"Silence!" Father Marlas said loudly.

With everything suddenly quiet he turned to me. His tone softened.

"Marko," he said and he seemed to be pleading a little. "Marko, you must understand."

Suddenly a great bitterness assailed me, and anger at myself, and a terrible sadness that flowed like night through my body because I could not make them understand.

"Father," I said quietly, "I am not a fool. I am Marko Palamas and once I pinned the mighty Zahundos in Baltimore. But this battle, more important to me by far, I have lost. That which has not the grace of God is better far in silence."

I turned to leave and it would have ended there.

"Hoodlum!" Uncle Paul said. "It is time you were silent!"

I swear in that moment if he had been a younger man I would have flung him to the dome of the church. Instead I turned and spoke to them all in fire and fury.

"Listen," I said. "I feel no shame for the violence of my feelings. I am a man bred of the Spartan earth and my emotions are violent. Let those who squeak of life feel shame. Nor do I feel shame because I saw this flower and loved her. Or because I spoke at once of my love."

No one moved or made a sound.

"We live in a dark age," I said. "An age where men say one thing and mean another. A time of dwarfs afraid of life. The days are gone when mighty Pindar sang his radiant blossoms of song. When the noble passions of men set ablaze cities, and the heroic deeds of men rang like thunder to every corner of the earth."

I spoke my final words to Ariadne. "I saw you and loved you," I said gently. "I told you of my love. This is my way—the only way I know. If this way has proved offensive to you I apologize to you alone. But understand clearly that for none of this do I feel shame."

I turned then and started to the door. I felt my heart weeping as if waves were breaking within my body.

"Marko Palamas," Ariadne said. I turned slowly. I looked at her. For the first time the warmth I was sure dwelt in her body radiated within the circles of her face. For the first time she did not look at me with her eyes like glaciers.

"Marko Palamas," she said and there was a strange moving softness in the way she spoke my name. "You may call on me tomorrow."

Uncle Paul shot out of his chair. "She is mad too!" he shouted. "He has bewitched her!"

"A disgrace!" Mr. Langos said.

"Call the police!" Uncle Paul shouted. "I'll show him if it's my business!"

"My poor daughter!" Mr. Langos wailed.

"Turk!" Uncle Paul shouted. "Robber!"

"Please!" Father Marlas said. "Please!"

I ignored them all. In that winged and zestful moment I had eyes only for my beloved, for Ariadne, blossom of my heart and black-eyed flower of my soul!

ZENA DAWN

THERE WAS a sound Zena Dawn heard early in the morning before daylight. In the beginning she thought it belonged to a dream but afterwards there were many nights she lay awake and heard it too. As if a strange wind, restless and cold, swept fleetingly through her room. But her door was closed and a ventilator locked in her single window. There was no opening through which a draft might enter.

Once she heard the sound she could no longer sleep. She drew the spread tightly to her throat and held herself aware of each long and silent minute.

The night is so long, she thought. The night is so quiet. Even a sudden fall of rain against the window comes as a relief. Even the murmur of the pigeons mourning in the cornices and the cry of a prowling cat help me remember I am not alone.

She was grateful for Mrs. Cohen's husband, a baker who rose early, a heavy-bodied man who tried to walk quietly. But his bulk and the absence of carpeting on the stairs defined his steps. His passing raised a shade on the night and soon the first in a series of alarm clocks ruffled the silence with a thin and agitated humming. A baby in the flat above hers wailed a hungry cry for food. Zena Dawn was able to sleep again knowing that the long night was over.

She woke to full daylight and the strong loud voice of Clara calling to her from the basement landing of the building next door. She rose from her bed and slipped into her robe feeling the stiff twinges of pain. She walked unsteadily to the window and raised the shade and waved.

Clara was a rampart-breasted Negro woman in her late fifties who owned the junk shop in the basement of the building next door. She lived in three rooms in the back of the store with a half-dozen children she raised alone since her husband deserted her.

"Good Lord!" Clara hollered and her voice carried clearly through the ventilator in the window. "Woman, you going to stay in bed all day? I'm on my third pot of coffee and the sweet rolls from Jenny is dripping sugar. Now put out the cups and I'm coming."

Zena Dawn turned eagerly from the window anticipating the visit which was a morning ritual for them both. She went to the mirror over the dresser and combed her hair. As she swept the strands back from her cheeks she saw how illness had ravaged her face and hidden her eyes in dark and solemn pits. She turned quickly from the mirror and walked to the small table that she covered with a clean cloth. From the shelf above the table she took down a pair of decorative cups and saucers. She had only a moment left to fill a pitcher with milk when she heard the heavy step of Clara on the stairs.

Clara entered like a wild woman clutching a pot of

steaming coffee in one hand and a bag of sweet rolls in the other.

"Gangway!" Clara cried. "On the way up here I run over two hags and burned hell out of a third!" She laughed boisterously and went rapidly to the table and poured the hot black coffee into the cups. She set the pot down on the small hot plate. "Get it while it's hot!" She waved Zena Dawn to the table and briskly opened the bag. "And wait till you taste them sweet rolls."

Zena Dawn sat down and placed the napkin carefully across her lap. "It smells good," she said. "Clara, the coffee certainly smells good this morning."

"You say that every morning," Clara said.

"I mean it every morning," Zena Dawn shook her head earnestly. "But this morning it smells especially good."

Clara tore a sweet roll in half with her big hands and took a large bite. She chewed vigorously and swallowed with pleasure. "Course it smells good," she said. "Clara Sullivan makes the best damn coffee in the city."

From the sidewalk below the window came a shrill cry.

"Can't leave me alone a minute," Clara said in a vexed voice. She walked from the table and flung open the window impatiently.

"Ma," the voice of her eldest boy called. "Ma, a man here wants to buy the iron eagle. I told him it was two dollar and he say he not going to give no more than one dollar."

"One dollar!" Clara hollered. "You tell that man that eagle belonged to a lady so rich and elegant I be ashamed to sell it for cheap pickings like one dollar. You tell him I rather throw it away or give it to one of you kids for a wedding present when you old enough to marry."

"He hear you, Ma," the boy called. "He putting on his hat."

"Wait!" Clara shouted. "Tell him if he pleased to pay a dollar and a half he can take that fine eagle home right now."

"He going, Ma," the boy said. "He got one foot out the door and the other in the air."

"Tell him to leave that dollar!" Clara screamed and her broad rump shook in agitation. "Get that dollar and give him the eagle. Clyde, you hear me! You make that sale or I beat your seat with a barrel stave. You hear!"

An anxious moment of silence passed and then the boy's voice floated up in triumph. "I got the dollar, Ma. The man got the eagle."

Clara drew her head back in and closed the window down to the ventilator loudly.

"That boy be my death," she said and returned to the table. "I try to teach him all I know and make a trader out of him but he don't know which end is up." She motioned at Zena Dawn's plate. "All that time," she said grievously. "You make only one chintzy little bite into that delicious sweet roll. You got to keep up your strength, honey, you all bones now."

"I'm not hungry," Zena Dawn said. "I love the sweet rolls but I'm just not hungry." She looked anxiously at Clara wishing to please her but unable to make the food go down her throat.

"You had much pain again?" Clara asked in a softer voice. "Did you pass another real bad night?"

"The pain wasn't bad at all last night," Zena Dawn said, and tried to speak cheerfully. "When I fell asleep I had a dream. I was somewhere in the sunshine, Clara, and could smell fresh flowers just as real as if I stood in a garden."

"The way you dream," Clara marveled. "And the things you dream."

"When I was a little girl I used to dream of flowers too," Zena Dawn said. "My father would kiss me goodnight and I would smell the flowers of his shop on his clothes and our house was always full of flowers." She paused and looked shyly at her pale fingers on the cloth of the table. "I've told you so many times before."

"Tell me again!" Clara said. "I like for you to tell me again!"

"Our house was full of flowers," Zena Dawn said. "Roses and sunflowers and chrysanthemums. Clara, it was always so beautiful."

"I bet it was," Clara said in awe. "You were lucky." She clucked her tongue. "Flowers all the time. Imagine that."

"I loved my mother," Zena Dawn said, "but my father was more dear. He picked out my name. He called me Zena Dawn because it sounded like the name of a flower."

"It sure does," Clara agreed earnestly.

"He said my name would always be a charm," Zena Dawn said, "I would have many friends and people to love and I would never be lonely." She grew suddenly pensive. "That was so long ago. Mother died when I was still living at home. But when my father died I was far away and I rode a train for two days and a night to go to his funeral but when I got there they had buried him. And all the flowers were wilted too."

"Eat some of that sweet roll now," Clara said vigorously. "You listen to me and eat some of that sweet roll."

"Bawl me out, Clara," Zena Dawn smiled. "It makes me feel good when you bawl me out. When I get better and can sew again I will make you a dress, a beautiful red dress that you can wear to church on Sundays. I promise you that."

"A red dress?" Clara said pleased. "It's been a long time since Clara had a new dress." She winked at Zena Dawn.

"That's the way to talk," she said. "Think on tomorrow instead of what happened years ago."

"It's hard sometimes," Zena Dawn said. "How different we expect things to be. I was married to Theron for only three years when he was killed. He will be dead nineteen years this September. We had so short a time together. And the years have passed so quickly since then."

"We both lost our men," Clara said. "But your man went to heaven and my man just went." She paused and shook her head. "I married a real prize. I waited and thought carefully and then I picked the laziest, most no-count man I could find and I married him. He was big and sassy and loved to slap me across the seat." She laughed huskily in spite of herself. "But he was no good out of bed. He was an evil man that done every sin you can think of and even made up a few more." She sighed with pleasure in the recollection. "One day he up and left me. He left me with six kids. That man was evil and no good but for a long time I missed him. To this day whenever I smell cheap gin I think of him."

She rose from the table and carried the cups and saucers to the small sink. Zena Dawn rose to help her and a sharp quick pain in her body made her cry out.

Clara watched her in concern. "When is the doctor coming back?"

Zena Dawn sat down again and placed her hands with the fingers open squarely upon the cloth of the table. She breathed slowly and fearfully against the pain rippling within her. "He won't be back until the day after tomorrow. He told me to keep taking the pills."

"That's right," Clara said firmly. "Keep taking them medicines. They help you get better and keep the pain from becoming too bad." She peered closely at the assortment of bottles on the shelf. "You got any of them red pain killers left?"

"I've got some left," Zena Dawn said.

"When you run out I send Clyde to get you some more," Clara said.

"I won't let you spend any more money on me!" Zena Dawn said. "You have your own family and all the other things you do for me is enough."

"You just shut up," Clara said with rough tenderness. "When you well enough to begin to sew, you can pay me back." She stared sharply at Zena Dawn. "Any of the relief money left?" she asked. "Now don't tell me no lie."

"Only the rent money," Zena Dawn said. "Mr. Mitchell is coming for that tomorrow."

"Then he be here tomorrow," Clara said grimly. "He come on his black horse and with his black pocketbook open as wide as a whale's mouth. He come blowing his rent-horn like a wild jackass out of hell." She stopped pleased as Zena Dawn began to laugh. "It's true!" Clara cried vigorously to encourage the laughter. "If the Lord took it into his mind to wipe out the earth with forty days and forty nights of rain, just before we all drown, that bastard come swimming by for his rent."

Zena Dawn laughed so hard she had to hold her ribs. Clara watched her with pleasure. "Laugh!" Clara said fiercely. "Laugh! When you most feel like crying, that's the time to laugh!"

"Clara, Clara," Zena Dawn said in wonder as she caught her breath. "How can you laugh when you've got the children to worry about, to feed and to clothe, and the store to run, and me to look after?"

"I got a few more things even than that," Clara said with a tight edge to her voice. "I got a boy whose teeth coming in so crooked they look like they belong in two different mouths. Doctor says he needs wires around them and for the price I swear I could buy ten miles of fence. And I got two feet, two damn feet that raise corns and calluses quicker'n the landlord can raise the rent. And I just got a letter from my daughter, the growed-up one, that married the iceman. He beating her up every Saturday night now and she want to bring her baby and stay with me."

"O Clara," Zena Dawn said in quick compassion. "I'm so sorry for her."

"That's all right," Clara shook her head with a savage resolve. "I told her to come. We make room for her and the baby. Always room for a few more." She brushed the crumbs from the bodice of her dress and looked sternly at Zena Dawn. "Now you do like you're supposed to," she said. "I'll see you a little later."

Zena Dawn was silent for a moment. She struggled for words to encompass the measure of Clara's devotion. Clara cut off her need to speak with a quick wave of her broad-palmed hand.

"There ain't no need to say nothing," Clara said. "As for looking after you, I do that because I want to. Maybe," she shrugged wryly, "maybe because you're a white woman and there ain't no white man nor white woman showed up to help you." She smiled in a gentle jest. "Maybe it's just your fancy name. Zena Dawn. Maybe that's it. You got to live fifty-seven years with a washerwoman name like Clara to understand that." She picked up the coffee pot and started briskly to the door. She paused with her hand upon the knob. "You call me now if you get bad pain," she said. "Just holler by the window."

When she had gone, Zena Dawn felt as if all the light and life in the room had fled as well.

At lunch Clara sent her a bowl of soup and some crackers which she barely managed to finish. Later Clyde brought up the afternoon paper. Zena Dawn read for a while and in the late afternoon the sharp stabbing pain returned. She went quickly to the bed and pressed her arms tightly across her stomach. She held her breath because she could feel the walls crumbling again, the tissue-thin walls that gave way before the bleeding. She felt her life draining out with her blood. She managed to rise from the bed and with a faint cry of despair stumbled to the ledge above the table and took down one of the bottles of pills. With a flare of panic she noted only one was left. She filled a glass with water and flooded it down. She went back to the bed and lay down and pressed her face into the pillow.

She felt a pounding in her forehead, an ache behind her eyes. Her breath rose in little bubbles to pop in her ears.

How lightly I lie upon the springs, she thought, how fragile is my hold upon the earth. A gust of strong wind could blow me away. She turned on her back and stared gravely at the ceiling. It was blue by day but in the twilight all color seemed bled from it, and it loomed over her head as if it were the cold stone of a tomb.

She tried furiously to form the images of memories. Once when I was a child, she thought. But she could go no further. One memory fell upon another. One tumbled quickly upon the next. They would not assemble into any order.

A minute passed and then another. Or was it an hour? She fell asleep. A great starburst of pain woke her. She shrieked and pulled at the sheet. Despair flooded over her. She cried out to her father. The room door opened and Clara stormed in.

"Damn you," Clara said. "I told you to call me. Damn you, white woman, with your fancy name!" Then in quick remorse she raised the slim frail body and held her fiercely to her own great breasts and rocked her gently back and forth.

"Clara!" Zena Dawn cried and she looked in terror at the ceiling. "I want to go to the hospital. Maybe they can help me there."

"Just hold up," Clara said. "There ain't nothing the hospital can do for you that old Clara can't do."

"Don't leave me alone," Zena Dawn whispered. "Clara, don't leave me alone. I am dying and don't leave me alone."

"Only a minute, honey," Clara said in a soft and shaken voice. "Only one minute to phone the doctor and I'll come back and I won't leave you again."

THE DOCTOR came a few hours later. He sat beside the bed and briefly examined Zena Dawn. She watched him from her eyes that were crusted by pain. He filled a syringe and gave her a shot. He closed his bag and rose to leave. Clara followed him to the hall outside the door.

The doctor looked tired and out of sorts. "Something might keep her alive a few more days," he said. "But it's better if she goes fast." He turned away and Clara caught at his sleeve.

"She wants to go to the hospital," Clara said. "She thinks they might help her there."

"That won't do any good," the Doctor said quietly.

A sudden anger flared in Clara's voice. "They don't want her to die there," she said. "They want poor folks to do their dying at home."

"Everybody is dying, mother," the Doctor said. "The rich and the poor and the weak and the strong. Everybody is dying a little all the time."

"I know," Clara said and her anger left as quickly as it had come. "God knows that is the truth."

She sat with Zena Dawn through the night. In the dark still hours after midnight she rose at intervals from her chair beside the bed and stretched against the stiffness cramping her body. She went a number of times to the window and listened for a sound from the basement next door.

Zena Dawn stirred uneasily on the bed and Clara took her a little water and moistened her lips. Her face was loose and dark, changed somehow, and her lips trembled in drugged and uneven sleep.

The hours passed slowly. Standing by the window Clara heard the cooing of the pigeons in the cornices. Somewhere a dog barked a sharp sound upon the night. She sat down in the chair and closed her eyes and dozed. Mrs. Cohen's husband woke her as he left for work, his steps heavy and clear upon the stairs. An alarm clock hummed down the long corridor. A baby raised a plaintive cry.

Clara walked to the window and raised the shade. The first faint gray of morning hung across the roofs of the city. A pigeon took flight with a harsh beating of its wings. She peered down at the back of her store to make sure everything was still quiet. She went back to the bed to cover Zena Dawn and saw how still she lay within the folds of sheet. Clara shook her head gratefully and pressed her hands tightly against her breasts.

The back door of the store downstairs opened and the voice of one of her children rose to her. She walked to the ventilator and called that she was coming. She turned for a moment back to the bed.

"You don't worry no more now, Zena Dawn," she said quietly. "You got a place all set for you. Old Clara been paying on a burial plot for you too, right next to me, and you don't worry no more now." She wiped fiercely at her eyes with the back of her hand. "There ain't going to be no more pain and no more bleeding and no more white folks not caring whether you live or die. Ain't going to be no more stale sweet rolls and no more landlord beating on the door come the first of the month. Ain't going to be no more relief checks that run out the end of the second week." She paused and struck her breasts violently with her fists. "You got a place next to me and they ain't going to put you in no pauper's grave nor cut you up. You got a place to rest and long as I live I see there is a flower on your head." She finished and shook her head in despair. "You the lucky one now," she said. "The rest of us got to go on living."

From the store another child wailed for her and a second took up the chorus of complaint. She turned and walked to the door. She looked back once and made a mute final gesture of consolation toward the body of Zena Dawn.

THE PRISON

HARRY KLADIS met Alexandra when he was forty-five and
she was forty. For twelve years he had worked with his
father in their small candy store. She was a librarian at
the neighborhood branch. He admitted to himself that
she was not very pretty and a little older than he would
have wished but he was drawn to her by the soft abundance
of dark hair that she wore to her shoulders and by an air
of shyness he suspected concealed loneliness as distressing
as his own. One night after she had been coming into
the candy store for almost three months, he mustered the
courage and asked to take her out. He was so pleased when
she accepted that he insisted she take three pounds of
her favorite chocolate mints as a gift.

On their first date they walked for hours and talked endlessly. In the beginning they tried shyly to suggest they
were accustomed to dating many others. After a while this

posturing seemed foolish to both of them. He told her
about a girl, handsome and raven-haired, that he had lost
to a bolder man years before. She told him of a salesman,
tall with sensitive eyes, who held her devotion until trans-
ferred to another territory he ceased to answer her letters.
These melancholy recitals drew them together. They were
delighted to find they both enjoyed concerts and chop suey
with black pekoe tea and almond cookies. After a month
of seeing each other several evenings a week they accepted
with grateful happiness that they were in love.

Two weeks before the day scheduled for their wedding,
Harry's father died. Returning from an evening with Alexandra, Harry found the old man in the back room of the
store where he had suffered a stroke while mixing a batch
of fresh milk chocolate.

They recognized it would have been unseemly to marry
so close upon death and they delayed their wedding for
a few months. Harry wished to sell the store as soon as
possible. He had studied accounting some years before
and considered taking additional courses to qualify himself
for that profession. But his mother insisted he keep the
thin security of the store that was all her husband had left
to provide for her old age. The first weeks after the funeral
seemed merely to sharpen the blades of her sorrow.

"My father and I were all she ever cared for," Harry
said to Alexandra. "He is gone now but she wonders what
will happen to me if I sell the store and cannot make a go
of accounting."

"You will be a good accountant," Alexandra said. "I
have my job to help out. It will be better for your mother
in the long run."

"I should have made the decision years ago," Harry said
and he was ashamed. "I never really cared for the store

but I have let the years slide by." He turned away to conceal his distress. "Just a while longer," he said. "I don't want to press Mama in her grief now. Just a little longer."

But he could not make chocolates as well as his father and business fell off. The price he might have received for selling the store declined as well. He worried and worked for longer hours. At the end of six months from his father's death they postponed their wedding once more.

His mother's continued despair confused him and made him unhappy. They tried to include the old lady in the things they did but she did not care for music and could not stand the sight or smell of chop suey. In desperation to appease her relentless grief they spent most of their evenings at home with her. She talked ceaselessly of the past and of joining her husband in death to remove herself as a burden on Harry. He spent the evening assuring her of his love and devotion. The only moments he managed alone with Alexandra were during the brief period when he walked her home. Then bedeviled by the evening of his mother's lament, he had little to say. When he returned home, he had to listen to his mother stitch the final ornament on the hours before he could flee to bed.

"Sitting in with me instead of being out with her," his mother said and a long sigh came wracked from her flesh. "She must resent me and blame me."

"She does not blame you for anything, Mama," Harry said. "She has never spoken a single word against you."

"I want you to marry," his mother said. "I want you to be happy." She looked in dismay at her son. "You were our only child. You are my life now. I would swear to die tonight if you thought I did not want your happiness."

"Stop it now," Harry said. "When Alexandra and I are married, you will live with us and we will look after you."

The old lady shook her head somberly. "You were two years old when your father's sister Sophoula died," she said. "The last ten years of her life she lived with us. I bathed her and fed her and cleaned up her slop. I would say my prayers at night and ask God to forgive me because I hated her on my back and wished her dead." She paused and with her dark dried fingers made her trembling cross. "There were nights I would hear her calling to me," she said. "I would hold my ears and make off I was asleep. And she would call in a voice like a bird for a long time." She bared her teeth in a harsh and cold smile. "My sins have come home to roost. I am the old woman now."

"What more can I say, Mama?" Harry asked. "As long as I live I will love you and look after you. And Alexandra will love you as I do."

The old lady looked at him silently for a long time. He felt himself reduced to the condition of a child unaware of reality and the grim shades of life. She rose slowly and heavily to her feet.

Harry kissed her goodnight with tenderness. For a moment she clung to him fiercely. He felt her fear of death and loneliness riot through his own flesh.

WINTER passed into spring. The hours of daylight grew longer. From blossoming gardens in the park came the aroma of new flowers. Within the foliage of trees sounded the shrill-throated songs of birds. In the twilight the moths writhed their wings about the street lamps. The young lovers whispered and laughed in the sheltered groves beyond the walk.

With the coming of spring, Harry and Alexandra felt their spirits rising. Sunday afternoons they spent looking for an apartment with an extra bedroom. They talked confidently of the future. The season filled them with new strength.

On the last Sunday in April they found a bright apartment not far from the park and only a few blocks from the library and candy store. Alexandra was enchanted with it but Harry could not subdue his apprehension. He could already feel the dark somber attendance of his mother. And closing their bedroom door at night would not shut out her brooding presence.

Afterwards they walked silently in the park. They passed old men with bony faces who sat on benches like withered roosters soaking up the sun, old men who bore the marks of neglect and impending death.

"We will take the apartment!" Harry spoke in a furious effort to break free. "We will go back and take it."

"You did not want it," Alexandra said quietly. "We have been searching for a place like that for weeks and when we found it you did not want it."

He fumbled helplessly for her hand and felt her slim-boned fingers against his palm. "In every room I could feel my mother," he said. "Like all the curtains were drawn and the shades pulled down."

"She cannot live alone," Alexandra said. "We have to work it out."

"She is sure we will come to hate her," he said. "Maybe she is right. I love her and feel a terrible pity for her. I love you too and I don't know what to do."

They paused before a deserted bench and sat down. He put his arm around her slim shoulders and drew her close.

"When I found you I had given up hope of love," she said quietly. "I had put that dream away like a flower pressed between the pages of a book." She moved her head slightly and he felt her breath against his throat.

"Now I brush my hair as I did when I was a girl. Every mirror makes me realize I am no longer young. I want you to love me and find me beautiful. I want you to love me before I grow old."

"We will work things out," Harry said and for a moment tightly closed his eyes. "We won't lose each other. We will work things out."

Summer passed. The hours of daylight grew shorter. Dusk and dark advanced as the autumn nights closed in. The earth stirred and waited for the winter.

His mother grew more feeble. She could not bear to be alone and in the afternoon had a neighbor woman help her to the store. She sat in a corner and watched Harry as he worked. In the evening the neighbor returned and took her home so that she could prepare Harry's supper. She sat watching him silently as he ate.

Afterwards he helped put her to bed. She was driven with fear that death would claim her while she slept so she delayed sleeping as long as possible, holding Harry's hand, and talking aimlessly of the past. There were moments when she looked at her son with a strange burning pity. "There is no answer for us on this earth," she said and made her cross. "God save you by taking me soon."

After she slept Harry went to his bed on the couch in the next room and lay awake for a long time. Finally weary and tormented by his thoughts, he fell asleep.

IN DECEMBER of that year Harry and Alexandra parted. They had been seeing each other less frequently as the weeks passed, each meeting marked by a silent grievance and rebuke. They were lonely away from one another and yet miserable when they were together. He made the suggestion, trying to hold back his tears, and she mutely agreed.

That night Harry did not go home. He knew his mother would be in terror at being alone but he remained all night in the store and mixed more chocolate than he would be able to use in months. He kept all the lights burning and tried furiously to keep busy. In the dawn when weariness finally overcame him, he sank down on a chair and laid his head on the table smelling of sweet chocolate. In that moment he envied his father who was dead.

For almost three years Harry did not see Alexandra. From an acquaintance he knew she still worked at the library. He was often tempted to walk by the library in the hope of catching a glimpse of her. He was afraid she might see him and this kept him away.

He saw her often in his dreams. Her thin mournful face and the long hair about her pale cheeks and her slim fingers quiet in her lap. In the morning he woke unrested and faced the day with a burden on his heart.

His mother grew a little stronger. Now that she had him to herself she made fewer demands upon him and let him alone. They never spoke of Alexandra.

He had always been careful about his diet but as time went on he ate as much as wished and gained weight. When he shaved in the morning he was repelled at how suddenly he seemed to have aged. He was not yet fifty but he felt much older.

More and more the pattern of his life assumed the dimensions that had governed the last years of his father. He rose early and went to the store. He worked through the day and in the evening went home to eat the supper his mother prepared. Afterwards he sat and read the paper while she rocked silently in her chair. When she was in bed he smoked a cigar as furtively as his father had done because she had always complained about the rank odor. He had trouble sleeping and after a while began using sleeping pills that a doctor prescribed.

In the beginning of the fourth year after he and Alexandra separated, his mother died. A cold had plagued her for several weeks. She ran a high fever and had to be moved to the hospital. The fever blazed up and down in spurts while she struggled fiercely to live. A priest came and dispensed the last rites. She died late one night in her sleep.

AFTER THE funeral Harry returned to the flat alone. He walked slowly about her bedroom. Every possession of hers, every article of clothing or spool of thread seemed to belong to someone he could hardly remember. He felt suddenly as if she had been dead for a long time.

He went for a walk. Without awareness of direction he found himself across the street from the library. In a panic that Alexandra might see him for the first time in three years on the day of his mother's funeral, he fled back home.

In the next few days he kept thinking about Alexandra. He yearned to go to her and yet shame kept him away. He studied himself in the mirror and mourned how seedy he had become. He determined desperately to diet again and brushed his hair in a way that concealed the growing patch of baldness.

After closing the store in the evening he detoured on his way home to pass the library. He stood hidden in the darkness of the small park across the street. When she came out and started to walk home he knew that he still loved her and had always loved her.

One night that he stood beneath the shadow of the trees a longing to talk to her overcame his shame and fear.

When she emerged from the library he crossed the street and called out her name.

It was a strange moment. She did not seem surprised to find him there. He was stunned at the sight of her and the changes that three years had made. She looked much older than he remembered, the last traces of youth gone. He trembled knowing that he too had changed and that she might see her own ravages reflected in him.

They walked home together as they had done so many times in the past. He was careful not to walk too close beside her. For a block they were silent and then they spoke a little. She had become head librarian. He mentioned a concert he had attended a few months before.

They paused before her building. He was about to say goodnight and try and muster the courage to ask to see her again.

"Would you like some tea?" she asked quietly.

For a moment, choked by gratefulness, he could not speak. They walked slowly up the stairs. He sat in her small parlor while she heated water in the kitchen. Everything appeared the same. The rows of books and records in the corner, the photograph of her dead parents, the small plaster bust of Beethoven on the mantel. The room even retained the delicate scent of her powder and he leaned back slightly and closed his eyes. He felt for an overwhelming moment that he was back where he had always belonged.

She brought in the pot of tea and set the cups upon the small table. She poured carefully and filled a plate with a few almond cookies. He had not eaten them in years.

"Do you still like chop suey?" he asked gently.

She shook her head. "Not any more," she said. Her

hands, pale and slim-fingered, moved restlessly about the cups of fragrant tea.

"I don't care for it any more either," he said. He was silent a moment, wondering if he had suggested too much.

When he finished his tea he rose slowly to his feet. He wanted to stay longer and yet was afraid to ask.

She brought him his coat. "You have gained weight," she said.

He fumbled hurriedly into the concealment of the coat. "I have started to diet again," he said.

"Your cheeks have no color," she said. "And you are growing bald."

He made a mute and helpless gesture with his hands.

"Do you find me changed?" she asked and a certain tightness had entered her voice.

"Hardly at all," he said quickly. He was sorry the moment he uttered that naked lie.

"Three years have passed," she said and the words came cold from her lips. "I was not young when you first met me. I am much older now."

"Alexandra," he felt a furious need to console her. "Alexandra," he drew a deep breath and then could not control the wild tumble of words. "Can you care a little for me again? Can you let me love you once more?"

She made a stiff and violent motion of her arm to silence him. He was shocked at the fury blazing suddenly in her eyes.

"Three years are two words," she said. "Two words easy to say. But three years are a thousand lonely nights and a thousand bitter cups of tea and a thousand withered flowers."

She raised her hand and struck him hard across the cheek. "For the thousand lonely nights!" she said and the words came in flame. "For the thousand bitter cups of tea! For the thousand withered flowers!" She struck him again more savagely than before.

He turned then and fled. He went quickly out the door, down the stairs to the sidewalk, across the street into the darkened doorway of a closed store. He stood there seeing the dark reflection of his face in the glass and felt his heart as if it were about to burst. He began to cry, the tears running down his stinging cheeks. And he did not know in that terrible moment of despair whether he was crying for Alexandra or for himself.

MATSOUKAS

ON SATURDAY evening Lambos kept his small grocery open an hour longer than his usual closing time. This enabled his regular customers to buy a carton of milk or a loaf of bread for Sunday morning when he did not open until noon.

That Saturday evening near the end of November was a cold and desolate night, the black and mottled streets deserted of all living things except a prowling tomcat gliding furtively through the glow of a street lamp before disappearing again into the dark cave of an alley.

Only a fool would brave the wind and the cold, Lambos thought, and his legs ached as they always did by the end of his long day. He yearned suddenly for his bed in the quiet small room above the store. He turned the key in the door and snapped off the main lights leaving only a tiny bare bulb above the window and another dim light in the rear of the store.

Across the street a tattered awning flapped in the wind. A patch of moonlight broke abruptly upon a sheet of newspaper floating over the curb. The beam of a passing car swept the pyramids of cans in his window. A corner of a wrapping-paper sign on which he had lettered with black crayon and taped to the window had come loose and he bent and pressed the tape back into place, feeling the glass cold beneath his fingers.

He was startled by the figure of a man watching him from the sidewalk outside his window. Lambos peered through the glass to identify him but the small bulb did not allow sufficient light. Deciding unhappily that he was a customer expecting the store to be open, Lambos snapped the lock back and opened the door.

The small bell tinkled as the man entered, a gust of icy wind swirling about his legs. Lambos shivered and closed the door quickly. When he turned around the man was standing almost concealed in shadow. Lambos could only make out that he was small of build wearing a gray topcoat too light for the weather and a battered felt hat pulled rakishly to one side.

"I was just closing," Lambos said in annoyance. He turned to open the overhead lights.

"Don't bother," the man said and it seemed to Lambos the words came flippantly from his mouth. He turned and peered over the counter at the shelves of canned goods. "Do you carry Meyer's clam chowder?" he asked.

"The supermarket in the next block," Lambos said brusquely. "They carry everything. I carry what my customers buy."

The man walked past the glass counter that contained several varieties of cheese. He halted before the small barrel of briny pickles. "These are my favorite," he said with a pleased wave. For a moment the light shone full across his face. He had a face shaped like a total moon with small bright eyes above the pinches of scarlet where the cold had marked his cheeks. His mouth was so wide when he smiled the corners cut almost to his nostrils giving him a droll and absurd appearance. Almost midnight, Lambos thought bitterly, and I get a clown.

"One pickle," the man said. "Mark it down." He reached into the barrel and raised a single dripping pickle and with measured relish bit off the end.

"I will remember," Lambos said. "Something else?"

The man chewed the pickle slowly punctuating each bite with a loud smacking of his lips.

"A man shouldn't eat pickles this time of night," Lambos said. "They cause heartburn."

When there was still no answer, Lambos felt a sudden uneasiness. He looked toward the battered register in which he kept change and a few bills. As if understanding, the man laughed softly. "Don't worry about that, Lambos," he said.

"You know my name?" Lambos asked in surprise. He peered more closely at the man again.

The man finished the pickle and drew out a handkerchief to wipe his fingers. "You have never seen me before, Lambos," he said with a jaunty wink, "but you and I have had an appointment for a long time."

"Maybe you are right," Lambos said soothingly, "but it is late now, friend, and I wish to close up. If there is nothing else . . ."

Instead of moving toward the door, the man walked to the end of the counter. He sat down on a wooden crate and indolently crossed his legs. "That supermarket has ruined you, hasn't it?" he asked cheerfully.

"My business is no concern of yours," Lambos bristled, forgetting his decision to humor the man. He turned his back on him and picked up the broom and began sweeping a patch of floor in agitation. He heard no sound but the whisking of the strands of straw against the bare wood. He ceased sweeping and turned to stare helplessly at the man who had not moved.

"My name is Matsoukas," the man said and his mouth twisted in a weird and expansive grin.

Lambos saw a glimmer of hope. "Are you Greek?"

"What else?" Matsoukas said.

"If you are Greek," Lambos said, "you know it is not polite to enter a man's store at closing time and eat a pickle and sit around like you are in a coffeehouse."

"Think of me as a friend," Matsoukas said, "who has come to help you find rest."

"Five minutes after you are gone, friend, I will be in bed," Lambos said.

"You need a much longer rest," Matsoukas said. "A rest sleep for a single night cannot provide." He lifted his shoulders in a wry shrug. "Actually I've been putting this visit off. I should have come a year ago."

"Who are you?" Lambos said. "What do you want?"

The cold eyes measured him and the great mouth taunted him silently.

Lambos loosed a hoarse cry and walked as quickly as his legs would allow behind the counter. He reached into the box where he kept a hammer and raised it violently above his head.

"You are a crazy man!" he shouted. "Now get out of my store!"

Matsoukas pointed to the hammer and shook in a spasm of silent and sardonic laughter. "Cuckoo, cuckoo, cuckoo," he snickered when he could get his breath.

Lambos lowered the hammer slowly to the counter. "I don't understand," he said helplessly.

Matsoukas leaned forward and his face entered the ray of light. The mask of the clown was strangely altered, as if the surface were a dried and wrinkled crust stretching over something more ominous beneath.

"I will make it clear," Matsoukas said with disdain. "Your heels are run down, your cuffs shabby, your pants so stiff with odors even the moths ignore them." His voice was the jagged edge of a broken mirror. "Your veins are scurvy roads that run through the ruins of your body. You endure a solitude reserved for beasts and saints. It is time to throw in your soiled towel."

Lambos stared at him numbly trying to find some sense in what was happening. "Are you sure you are Greek?" he asked finally.

"My name is Matsoukas."

"A name means nothing."

"Mine does," Matsoukas chuckled.

"What does it mean?"

"What I want it to mean."

"I don't want to listen to you any more," Lambos said.

"You are not listening now," Matsoukas said harshly. "Protoplasm is a sticky business. Better to have it over and done with."

"Are you a doctor?" Lambos shook his head fitfully. "You want to take my temperature and give me a prescription? I have a cabinet full of powders and pills."

"It is too late for pills," Matsoukas said. "I am here to unchain you from your barrel of pickles. Wise up."

"Who are you?" Lambos cried. "Tell me who you are?"

"Who I am doesn't matter," Matsoukas said loudly. "It's who you are that counts."

"Who am I?" Lambos asked loudly.

"I can sum up your life in one breath," Matsoukas said. "First a suckling baby, then a child answering his name, a youth with pustules on his face, a man searching for love, a husband in the misery of unhappy marriage, a father dreaming of eternity and resurrection," his baleful eyes flayed Lambos with scorn. "Now you are a sick and spindly-legged old man, wife and son dead, and not a single reason why you shouldn't be too. Wise up."

"Leave me alone." Lambos put his hands desperately to his ears.

"Admit what I say is true," Matsoukas said. "Is there anyone left to mourn you? Is there anyone left to love you?" He made a gesture of impatience. "I can't waste much more time here." He rose from the crate and walked in agitation to stand at the window staring silently into the street.

"Listen to me," Lambos pleaded. "Will you listen to me?" When Matsoukas did not turn around, Lambos began to pace the store. "How can you know what I am?" he said. He started around the counter and turned and walked back, dragging one foot slightly behind him. "Twenty years I was married," he said, "and then long after I had given up hope I could ever be a father, we had a son. All my life seemed different then." He passed beneath the light and bumped the edge of the counter and nearly fell. "I saw him growing into a fine man, raising a family of his own, my grandchildren. I saw my old age as green and warm. But from his tenth year he had a sickness in his body. For two years they kept him alive by giving him blood. He grew thin and his flesh bruised and blue and then he died. For two years I watched and measured each pulse of his dying. Not a day or night when I would not have died in his place." He paused and stretched his arms to the ceiling of the store and spread his dry stiff fingers, and then he cried out, a terrible cry of loss and despair. At the window Matsoukas stirred uneasily.

Lambos walked wearily to the same crate Matsoukas had used a short while before. He sat down and let his face drop slowly against his cupped hands. He closed himself into the nest of his palms, alone for a moment with the heavy beating of his heart. "I am afraid," he said softly. "I am afraid."

Matsoukas turned then from the window. He walked to Lambos and then slowly and awkwardly put out his hand and touched Lambos gently on the shoulder.

"Listen, Lambos," Matsoukas spoke in a strangely altered voice. "Your heart is scarred by loneliness and sorrow. Your body is a wound from which your life falls like drops of blood. Your burden is hopeless and it will grieve no one if you lay it down."

Lambos closed his eyes tightly for a long moment. When he opened them he noticed that moonlight had entered the store. It shimmered across the worn wood of the floor and swirled mist in the corners.

"It is easy to accomplish," Matsoukas said. "Merely believe and say, I want to die. Think of night eternal across your body." He paused and drew a fitful breath. "I'll tell you something I don't ever bother to tell anyone. Grief and despair belong to life. False dreams and vain hopes belong to life. Death is peace."

It seemed to Lambos in that moment as if the sharp and mournful world around him began to soften. The edges began to dissolve, shelves and counters and walls fading slowly away.

Lambos nodded slowly and rose. He hesitated for a moment and then reached again for the broom. He swept the last of the litter into a pile and picked it up with a piece of cardboard that he threw into the basket in the corner. Then he fumbled at the apron that bound his waist.

"When I was a boy I had such dreams," Lambos said.

He looked sadly around the store. "Now at the end there is so much I do not understand," he sighed, "perhaps if I had not been such a simple man . . ."

"Only the simple and the great may be sure of dying in their own way," Matsoukas said. "The rest die in imitation."

Lambos folded his apron and placed it upon the counter. He stood uncertainly for a moment as if there were something he had forgotten to do. "Will you stay with me now?" he asked and tried not to show his fear.

"Each man must enter death for himself," Matsoukas said. "But do not despair, Lambos. Go up to your bed and lie down and close your eyes and you will sleep as you have never slept before. I promise you that."

Lambos walked to the foot of the steps. He looked once to the door at the top and then turned back to Matsoukas.

"And God?" he asked softly. "Where is God in all of this?"

"If you have not found the answer to that in all your years on earth," Matsoukas said gravely, "how can you expect to have the answer now?"

Lambos placed his hands on the railings for balance and started slowly up. He heard the tinkling of the bell above the door and felt a sudden gust of wind about his legs. He looked back and beyond the glass of the window saw the arm of Matsoukas raised in a shadowed farewell.

He walked up a few more steps. The chill of stone crept into his body and he thought of tombs and the comfortless earth. He remembered his son and tried to go higher but his one leg trembled so badly it would not hold him.

"Matsoukas!" he cried.

There was no answer from the store below him. The steps he had passed were shrouded in darkness. He looked once more up to the door and felt himself suspended on a frail bridge over the void. He slipped to one knee.

"Matsoukas!" he cried in anguish. "Help me!"

Then he remembered. Grief and despair belong to life, Matsoukas had said, false dreams and vain hopes belong to life. Death is peace.

He pulled himself to his feet and holding to the railing with both hands began to drag himself up. Strangely his fear was gone and he felt a strength such as he had not felt in many years. He smelled the fragrance of his unmarked youth, the childhood of his life. He felt with certainty that he was going home, mind and body and heart back to his beginning.

His voice echoed in a long joyous cry down the stairs. Below him the shelves and pyramids of cans, the racks of bread and the paper banners, snapped squarely and forever into darkness.

THE JOURNAL
OF A WIFE-BEATER

OCTOBER 2: Today I beat my wife, Nitsa, for the first time! I preserve this momentous event for future generations by beginning this Journal and recording this first entry with some pride.

I did not beat her hard, really not hard at all. I gave her several clouts across her head with my open palm, enough to make her stagger and daze her a little. Then I led her courteously to a chair to show her I was not punishing her in anger.

"Why?" she asked, and there were small tears glistening in the corners of her eyes.

"Nothing of great significance," I said amiably. "The coffee you served me was not hot enough this morning and after the last few washings my shirts have not had enough starch. Yesterday and the day before you were late in arriving at the restaurant. All of these are small imprudences that display a growing laxity on your part. I felt it was time to suggest improvement."

She watched me with her lips trembling. How artfully women suffer!

"You have never struck me before," she said thoughtfully. "In the year since we married, Vasili, you have never struck me before."

"One does not wish to begin correction too soon," I said. "It would be unjust to expect a new bride to attain perfection overnight. A period of flexibility is required."

Her big black eyes brooded, but she said nothing.

"You understand," I said consolingly. "This does not mean I do not love you." I shook my head firmly to emphasize my words. "It is exactly because I do care for you that I desire to improve you. On a number of occasions in my father's house I can remember him beating my mother. Not hard you understand. A clout across the head, and a box upon the ear. Once when she left the barn door open and the cows strayed out, he kicked her, but that was an exception. My mother was a happy and contented woman all her life."

The conversation ended there, but Nitsa was silent and meditative as we prepared for bed. She did not speak again until we were under the covers in the darkness.

"Vasili," she asked quietly, "will you strike me again?"

"Only when I feel you need it," I said. "It should not be required too often. You are a sensible girl and I am sure are most anxious to please me by being a good wife and a competent homemaker."

She turned away on her pillow and did not say another word.

OCTOBER 3: I slept splendidly last night!

OCTOBER 5: Since I have a few moments of leisure this evening, I will fill in certain background information about Nitsa and myself so that future generations may better understand this record of an ideal marriage relationship.

First I must record my immense satisfaction in the results of the beating. Nitsa has improved tremendously the past two days. She has taken the whole affair as sensibly as any man could have wished.

Her good sense was what first impressed me about Nitsa. I met her about a year ago at a dance in the church hall, sponsored by the daughters of Athens. I drank a little beer and danced once with each of a number of young ladies whose zealous mothers beamed at me from chairs along the wall. I might add here that before my marriage a year ago I was a very desirable catch for some fortunate girl. I was just a year past forty, an inch above average height, with all of my own hair and most of my own teeth, a number of which have been capped with gold. I had, and of course still have, a prosperous restaurant on Dart Street and a substantial sum in United States Savings Bonds. Finally, I myself was interested in marriage to a well-bred young lady. My first inclination was to return to Greece and select some daughter born to respect the traditions of the family; but as our parish priest, Father Antoniou, pointed out with his usual keen discernment, this would have been grossly unfair to the countless girls in our community who hoped for me as a bridegroom. Although marriage to any one of them would dismay the others, it would be better than if I scorned them all for a wife from overseas.

Nitsa impressed me because she was not as young as most of the other girls, perhaps in her late twenties, a tall athletic-looking girl who appeared capable of bearing my sturdy sons. She was not as beautiful a girl as I felt I deserved, but she made a neat and pleasant appearance. Most attractive young girls are too flighty and arrogant. They are not sensible enough to be grateful when a successful man pays them attention. Bringing one of them into a man's home is much the same as bringing in a puppy that has not yet been housebroken. Too much time is spent on fundamentals!

Imagine my delight when, in inquiry regarding Nitsa's family that night, I learned she was the niece of our revered priest, Father Antoniou, visiting him from Cleveland.

I danced several American dances with her to demonstrate I was not old-fashioned and spoke to her at some length of my assets and my prospects. She listened with unconcealed interest. We sat and drank coffee afterward until a group of my friends called to me to lead one of the old country dances. Conscious of her watching me, I danced with even more than my usual grace and flourish, and leaped higher off the floor than I had in some time.

A day or two later I spoke seriously to Father Antoniou. He was frankly delighted. He phoned his sister, Nitsa's mother in Cleveland, and in no time at all the arrangements were made. As I had accurately surmised, the whole family, including Nitsa, were more than willing.

Several weeks later we were married. It was a festive affair and the reception cost a little over a thousand dollars which I insisted her father pay. He was a housepainter who worked irregularly, but in view of the fact that Nitsa brought me no dowry I felt he should demonstrate the good faith of the family by paying for the reception.

Nitsa and I spent a weekend at the Mortimer Hotel for our honeymoon, so I could return to count the cash when the restaurant closed each evening. As it was, God only knows what the waitresses stole from me those two days. During our absence I had the bedroom of my apartment painted, and after considerable deliberation bought a new stove. I write this as proof of my thoughtfulness. The stove I had was only twelve years old, but I am worldly enough to understand how all women love new stoves. If permitted by weak and easily swayed husbands they would trade them in on newer models every year.

In recalling our first year together, while it was not quite what I expected, I was not completely disillusioned. There was a certain boldness and immodesty about Nitsa which I found displeasing, but one must bear with this in a healthy young woman.

As time went on she spent a good part of the day with me in the restaurant taking cash. She became familiar enough with my business so that when the wholesale produce and meat salesman called she could be trusted to order some of the staple items. But I noticed a certain laxity developing, a carelessness in her approach to her responsibilities, and remembering my father's success with my mother, it was then I beat her for the first time.

I am pleased that it seems to have prompted unreserved improvement. Bravo, Vasili!

OCTOBER 7: It is after midnight and I am alone in the restaurant which is closed until morning. I am sitting at the small table in the kitchen and can hardly bear to write the shameful and disgraceful episode which follows.

Last night after returning from the restaurant I went to bed because I was tired. Nitsa came into the room as I was slipping under the covers. I had noticed a rather somber quietness about her all that day, but I attributed it to that time of the female month. When she had donned her night clothes and gotten into bed beside me, I raised my cheek for her to kiss me goodnight. She turned her back on me and for a moment I was peeved, but remembering her indisposition I turned off the lamp and said nothing.

I fell asleep shortly and had a stirring dream. I fought beside Achilles on the plains before Troy. I carried a mighty shield and a long sword. Suddenly a massive Trojan appeared before me and we engaged each other in combat. After I brilliantly parried a number of his blows he seemed to recognize he was doomed. He retreated and I pressed him hard. While we slashed back and forth, another Trojan rose beside me as if he had sprung from the earth, and swung his weapon at my head. I raised my shield swiftly but not quite in time and the flat of his sword landed across my head. The pain was so terrible I shrieked out loud, and suddenly the plains of Troy and the helmeted warriors were all swept away and my eyes exploded open to the sight of Nitsa bent over me, calmly preparing to strike again!

I bellowed and clawed to sit up, and tried desperately to flee from the bed. The stick she swung bounced again across my head and the pain was ferocious. I fell off the bed in a tangle of sheets at her feet; then I jumped up frantically and ran to the other side of the bed, looking back in desperation to see if she followed. She stood dreadfully calm with the stick still in her hand.

"Are you mad!" I shouted. My nose seemed to be swelling and my head stung and I tasted blood from my cut lip. "You must be mad or in the employ of the devil! You have split me open!"

"I owed you one," she said quietly. "A debt that had to be paid."

I looked at her in astonishment and rubbed my aching head. I could not comprehend the desecration of a wife striking her husband. "Your senses have come apart," I bellowed. "You might have broken my head!"

"I don't think so," she said. "You have an unusually dense head."

I was horrified. On top of my injuries her insolence could not be tolerated. I ran around the bed and pulled the stick from her hands. I swung it up and down. When it landed across her shoulders she winced and gave a shrill squeal. Then I went to bathe my swollen head. A harrowing and terrible experience indeed!

OCTOBER 11: Plague and damnation! Blood and unspeakable horror! She has done it again.

That wench of evil design waited just long enough for the swelling of my nose to recede and my lip to heal. All week she had been quiet and reserved. She came to work promptly and performed her duties efficiently. While I could never forget that night in bed when she struck me, I was willing to forgive. Women are by nature as emotionally unstable as dogs under the mad light of a full moon. But I am a generous man and in this foul manner was my generosity rewarded.

It happened shortly after the rush at lunch was over. The restaurant was deserted except for Nitsa at the register and the waitresses chattering beside the urns of coffee. I was sitting at the small table in the kitchen, smoking a cigar, and pondering whether to order short ribs or pork loins for lunch on Thursday. Suddenly I was conscious of an uneasy chill in the center of my back. A strange quick dread possessed me and I turned swiftly around and Nitsa was there. Almost at the same instant the pot she was swinging landed with a horrible clatter on my head. I let out a roar of outrage and pain, and jumped up holding my thundering head. I found it impossible to focus my eyes, and for a frenzied moment I imagined I was surrounded by a dozen Nitsas. I roared again in fear and anger, and ran to seek sanctuary behind the big stove. She made no move to follow me but stood quietly by the table with the pot in her hand.

"You must be mad!" I shrieked. "I will call the doctor and have him exchange your bloody head!"

The dishwasher, who had come from the back room where he had been eating, watched us with his great idiot eyes, and the waitresses, cousins of imbeciles, peered through the porthole of the swinging door.

"I owed you one," Nitsa said quietly. She put down the pot and walked from the kitchen past the awed and silent waitresses.

As I write this now, words are inadequate to describe my distress. Fiercer by far than the abominable lump on my head is the vision of chaos and disorder. In the name of all that is sacred, where is the moral and ordered world of my father?

OCTOBER 15: Disturbed and agitated as I have been for the past few days, tonight I decided something had to be done. I went to speak to Father Antoniou.

Nitsa, that shrew, has been at the restaurant for several days now acting as if nothing had happened. She joked with the customers and took cash calmly. Heartless wench without the decency to show some shred of remorse!

Last night I slept locked in the bathroom. Even then I was apprehensive and kept one eye open on the door. While it was true that by her immoral standards we were even, she could not be trusted. I feared she would take it into her stony soul to surge into a shameful lead. Finally tonight, because I knew the situation had become intolerable, I visited the priest.

He greeted me courteously and took me into his study.

He brought out a bottle of good sherry. We sat silent for a moment, sipping the fine vintage.

"You may speak now, my dear friend," he said gently. "You are troubled."

"How can you tell, Father?" I asked.

He smiled sagely. He was indeed a fountain of wisdom.

"Well, Father," I struggled for the mortifying words. "It is Nitsa. To put it plainly, she has struck me not once, but twice, with a stout stick and a heavy pot."

He sat upright in his chair.

"May God watch over us!" he said. "Surely, Vasili, you are jesting!"

I made my cross and bent my head to show him the hard lump that still dwelt there. He rose from his chair and came to examine it. When he touched the lump, I jumped.

He paced the floor in agitation, his black cassock swirling about his ankles.

"She must be demented," he said slowly. "The poor girl must be losing her mind."

"That is what I thought at first," I said seriously. "But she seems so calm. Each time she strikes she merely says, 'I owed you one.'"

"Aaaaah!" the priest said eagerly. "Now we approach the core of truth." His voice lowered. "What did you do to her for which she seeks revenge?" He winked slyly. "I know you hot-blooded Spartans. Perhaps a little too passionate for a shy young girl?"

"Nothing, Father!" I said in indignation, although I could not help being pleased at his suggestion. "Absolutely nothing."

"Nothing?" he repeated.

"I have clouted her several times across her head," I said.

"My prerogative as a husband to discipline my wife. Certainly nothing to warrant the violence of her blows."

"Incredible," the priest said. He sat silent and thoughtful, then shook his head. "A woman raising her hand to her husband in my parish, and that woman my niece. Incredible!" He wrung his hands fretfully. "A stain upon the sacred vows of marriage." He paused as if struck by a sudden thought. "Tell me, Vasili, has she been watching much television? Sometimes it tends to confuse them."

"Our picture tube is burned out now several months, Father," I said. "They want a fantastic price to fix it."

"Incredible," the priest said.

"Perhaps if you talk to her, Father," I said. "Explain what it is to be a dutiful wife. Define the rights of a husband."

The priest shook his head sadly. "When I first entered the priesthood," he said somberly, "I learned never to attempt to reason with a woman. The two words should never be used in the same sentence. The emancipation of these crafty scheming descendants of Eve has hurled man into a second Dark Ages."

I was impressed by the gravity of his words and had to agree I had spoken hastily.

"My son," the priest said finally, a thin edge of desperation in his voice. "I confess I am helpless to know what to advise. If you came to seek counsel because she drank to excess or because she had succumbed to the wiles of another man . . . but for this! I will have to contact the Bishop."

I sipped my sherry and felt anger coming to a head on my flesh as if it were a festered boil pressing to break. I, Vasili Makris, subjected to these indignities! Humiliated before my own dishwasher! Driving my parish priest to consult with the Bishop!

"There is only one answer, Father," I said, and my voice rang out boldly, a call to battle. "I have clouted her too lightly. There is nothing further to be done but for me to give her a beating she will not forget!" I waved my hand. "Rest assured I will remember my own strength. I will not break any bones, but I will teach her respect." I became more pleased with that solution by the moment. "That is the answer, Father," I said. "A beating that will once and for all end this insufferable mutiny!"

We watched each other for a long wordless moment. I could sense that good man struggling between a moral objection to violence and an awareness there was no other way.

"They who live by the sword," he said dolefully, and he paused to permit me to finish the quotation in my mind. "This cancer must be cut out," he said, "before it spreads infection through the parish."

Father Antoniou raised his glass and toasted me gravely.

"Consider yourself embarked on a holy crusade," he said in a voice trembling with emotion. "Recapture the sanctity of your manhood. Go, Vasili Makris, with God."

I kissed his revered hand and left.

OCTOBER 17: The promised retribution has been delayed because a waitress has been sick and I cannot afford to incapacitate Nitsa at the same time. But I vow her reprieve will be brief!

OCTOBER 19: Tonight is the night! The restaurant is closed and we are alone. I am sitting in the kitchen making this entry while she finishes cleaning out the urns of coffee. When the work is all done I will call her into the kitchen for judgment.

Nitsa! Misguided and arrogant woman, your hour of punishment is here!

OCTOBER 23: In the life of every noble man there are moments of decisive discovery and events of inspired revelation. I hasten with fire and zeal to record such an experience in this Journal!

That epic night when Nitsa came to the kitchen of the restaurant after finishing her work, without a word of explanation I struck her. Quick as a flash she struck me back. I was prepared for that and hit her harder. She replied with a thump on my head that staggered me. I threw all hesitation to the winds and landed a fierce blow upon her. Instead of submitting, she became a flame of baleful fury. She twisted violently in search of some weapon to implement her rage, and scooped up a meat cleaver off the block! I let out a hoarse shout of panic and turned desperately and fled! I heard her pounding like a maddened mare after me, and I made the door leading to the alley and bounded out with a wild cry! I forgot completely the accursed stairs and spun like a top in the air and landed on my head. I woke in the hospital where I am at present and X-rays have indicated no damage beyond a possible concussion that still causes me some dizziness.

At the first opportunity I examined myself secretly for additional reassurance that some vital part of me had not been dismembered by that frightful cleaver. Then I sat and recollected each detail of that experience with somber horror. A blow now and then, delivered in good faith, is one of the prerogatives of marriage. Malevolent assault and savage butchery are quite another matter!

However, as my first sense of appalled outrage and angry resentment passed, I found the entire situation developing conclusive compensations. I had fancied myself married to a mortal woman and instead was united to a Goddess, a fierce Diana, a cyclonic Juno! I realized with a shock of recognition that one eagle had found another, perched on Olympian peaks, high above the obscure valley of pigeons and sheep.

O fortunate woman! You have gained my mercy and forbearance and have proven to my satisfaction that you deserve my virile love and are worthy of my intrepid manhood!

Nitsa, rejoice! You need no longer tremble or fear that I will ever strike you again!

THE SONG OF
RHODANTHE

I WAS TWENTY-SEVEN years old that spring. Papa had still not given up hope that a man would be found to marry me. My brothers, Kostas and Marko and Niko, were married and had numerous children of their own. They were all concerned about me.

It was true that I wanted to be married. Papa had presented a number of men to me for my approval. I was not beautiful but neither was I so homely that I had to accept one of them. They were either too old or too loud or red-faced from drinking too much beer and wine. I think Papa grieved most about me when wine made him tearful. His only daughter, twenty-seven, and still unmarried. Friends who were bachelors drank and grieved with him. In the end they offered themselves as suitors to ease Papa's despair.

AFTER AN evening with one of them Papa waited for my decision. I told him I refused to accept such a man.

"You are twenty-seven years old!" he cried. "A daughter still unmarried at twenty-seven is a plague on a man's spirit. I cannot sleep for worrying about you. My health is breaking down. At the market everyone asks me, Panfelio, is your daughter married yet? Is she even engaged? I cannot bear much more."

"Yes, Papa."

"What was the matter with Gerontis?" he asked.

"He is too old," I said, "and his false teeth whistle when he speaks."

"You are too choosy!" Papa shouted. "Remember you are twenty-seven years old."

"Yes, Papa."

"What was the matter with Makris?" he asked. "He is a younger man than Gerontis."

"He is younger," I said. "But he greases his hair until it drips oil down his cheeks and he spent all evening telling me how he can crack open a crate with his bare hands."

"I can still crack open a crate with my bare hands," Papa shouted. "Your poor Mama was never the worse for it. You forget, my girl, you are twenty-seven years old."

"Yes, Papa."

ONE EVENING a week, my brothers brought their wives and children to our house to eat supper. The wives were red-cheeked with great bosoms and ate like contented mares. The house became a bedlam with children hanging from the lamps and chairs collapsing with a sound of thunder. We assembled at the table and bowed our heads and Papa said grace.

"We are grateful, O Lord, that we are well and together and for the food upon this table. Bring us together again next week and let there be a man for Rhodanthe among us. Amen."

When dinner was over and it was time to leave, each of the wives of my brothers kissed me benevolently on the cheek. One after the other my big brothers embraced me sadly and kissed me somberly. Every parting was a festival of grief. Poor Rhodanthe.

I told Papa goodnight and kissed him tenderly because I loved him very much. He was foolish sometimes and shouted a great deal but I knew how much he loved me too.

I went to my room and prepared for bed. I sat before the mirror and brushed my long hair. In those moments I fiercely felt a wish to be married and raise children of my own. Sometimes I thought I wanted that as much for Papa and Kostas and Marko and Niko as for myself.

THE LAST cold months of winter passed. The winds grew gentle. The rain fell during the night and in the daylight the earth smelled fresh as if it were awakened from a long sleep. One morning I saw a robin sitting on a branch of the cherry tree in our yard and I knew the spring had really come.

Each morning Kostas and Marko and Niko drove up in their trucks to have a cup of coffee while Papa ate breakfast. I knew they did that for me so that I would not feel too lonely during the day.

They sat around the kitchen table, big strong men that made the kitchen seem smaller than it really was. The cups looked tiny and fragile in their massive hands. They smoked cigars and spoke in loud gruff voices to each other. But they were soft and gentle when they spoke to me.

When they had left with Papa for the market, I washed the dishes and cleaned the house. I worked quickly and felt a glow in my cheeks.

Because that day was so beautiful I decided to take the bedding outside to air. I carried the sheets and blankets to the back yard and draped them across a line. When I finished hanging them up I was a little out of breath.

There was the sound of whistling in the alley in back of the yard and a young man appeared. He was striding along with his hands in his pockets and his head flung back and a wild jubilant whistling ringing from his lips. I had heard whistling before, even the strong bass whistling of my brothers, but never a sound like he made. It was as if the spring had burst into song. As if the first slim green buds and the blades of new grass and the soft fresh wind had suddenly found a voice. And I felt a strange wild tremor through my heart.

When he saw me standing there he paused. For a quick tight moment the whistling ceased. His hair was thick and dark and an untamed and errant curl glittered across his forehead. He smiled then and his smile was as reckless and daring as his whistle. Then he walked on quickly and the wild whistling rang out again. As the sound faded a terrible loneliness overcame me. I went quickly into the house.

That night at supper I broke a cup and spilled soup from the pot while pouring it into a bowl.

"What is the matter with you?" Papa said. "You are nervous as a cat tonight."

"Nothing is the matter, Papa," I said and felt a quick flame in my cheeks.

He cleared his throat and sighed heavily.

"It is not normal," he said somberly. "Twenty-seven years old and still unmarried. You will become sick."

"I will not become sick, Papa," I said. "Do not worry about me."

"How can I help worrying?" he said. "What kind of father would I be if I did not worry about my daughter, still unmarried at twenty-seven?" His lips quivered and he wiped a stray tear from his eye.

"Yes, Papa."

"You are too choosy!" he shouted. "You have not that right at your age. Gastis passed the market today. He asked how you were. He was taken with you. What in God's name was the matter with Gastis?"

"I have told you before, Papa," I said.

"Tell me again!" he shouted.

"His face is like one of his grapefruit," I said. "He never smiles. Whatever time of day you are with him always appears to be night."

Papa threw up his hands in despair.

"One is too young," he said. "And one is too old. One laughs like an idiot and one does not laugh enough. One is a banana and one is a grapefruit. I am telling you, my girl, I am losing patience!"

"Yes, Papa."

"What kind of man do you want?" he shouted again. "Tell me what kind of man you want?"

I paused for a moment in the doorway of the kitchen. A reckless excitement swept my tongue.

"I want a young man with dark hair," I said boldly. "And a wild dark curl across his forehead. A man who whistles and makes the earth burst into song."

Papa made his cross.

"What I have feared has come to pass," he said sadly. "You have become unbalanced."

"Yes, Papa," I said, and I ran back to him and kissed him gently. "Good night, Papa."

IN THE morning I could not wait for all of them to leave. They sat over their coffee for what seemed to be an eternity. Yet each time I looked at the clock I saw they were no later than they usually were.

When they had gone I ran to my room and carefully brushed my hair and tied it with my brightest ribbon. I touched my lips with a light red stain and pinched my cheeks. I went quickly downstairs and out the back door. A moment of panic seized me when I realized I could not just stand there waiting. I hurried back into the house and pulled the blankets from my bed and ran with them down the stairs. I had just finished hanging them across the line when I heard the sound of the whistling again.

He came down the alley just as he had the morning before. His head flung back and his legs walking with great strong strides and that wonderful wild whistle singing on his lips. My heart beat suddenly as if it were going to burst apart.

When he saw me he stopped. He smiled again, a perfect and riotous smile. I could not help myself and smiled back. He walked slowly to the fence and carelessly and with a supple grace leaned his elbows upon it and put his face in his hands.

"You live here?" he asked. And he had a deep man's voice but not nearly as harsh a voice as Papa had, and with revelry in it, unlike the voices of Marko and Kostas and Niko.

"Yes," I said.

"With your husband?" he asked slyly.

"With my father," I said quickly. "I am not married."

"Good," he said, and he smiled again and threw back his head and laughed a festival of tuneful laughter from his throat. "Good," he said again and then he waved goodby and started striding down the alley.

There were a dozen questions I wanted to call after him, a dozen things I wanted to say. I was ashamed because I had answered and yet I felt strange and alive for the first time in my life. I looked at the budding leaves and at the first blades of grass and at the early tulips and felt a fervent kinship with them.

The next morning it rained and I was in despair. I could not stand in the rain waiting for him to pass, or hang blankets on a line in the downpour. After a while I gave up hoping it would stop in time and consoled myself that the following morning the sun might shine again.

I finished the kitchen and wiped the last breakfast cups without spirit. I hung the dish towel upon the rack, and heard a light tapping at the window.

My heart leaped to my throat because he was there. He waved to me through the rain-smeared glass. I ran to the door and flung it open. He came in dripping from the rain and the dark curly hair matted upon his head.

"You are soaked!" I said. "You'll catch cold! I'll get a towel."

He took the clean towel from my hands and began briskly to dry his hair. He rubbed his cheeks with vigor and smiled and shook his head.

"You weren't in the yard," he said.

I looked at him helplessly.

"It was raining so hard," I said. "I wasn't sure you would come."

When I realized what I had said I put my hand quickly to my mouth. But he only laughed softly.

"The rain is nothing," he said. "I missed you."

We looked at each other and there was taunting merriment in his dark eyes. I tried to think of something to say but all my senses seemed to have fled.

"I've got to go in a minute," he said. "I'll be late for work."

"A cup of coffee," I said. "It's still hot. It will warm you."

He came to the table and he was not as tall as any of my brothers and not as broad in the shoulders as my father, but there was grace and strength in the way he moved.

I brought the pot of coffee to the table and filled his cup. I could sense him watching me and I spilled some into the saucer.

"Weren't you afraid to let me in?" he said.

I turned away quickly and shook my head.

"What's your name?" he said.

"Rhodanthe," I said. I put the pot back on the stove and then turned to face him.

"A pretty name," he said. "A name for a flower."

I looked down at the floor because I was sure the frantic beating of my heart would show in my cheeks.

"I know a great deal about you," he said and when I looked up he winked slyly. "I know more about you than you realize."

"You do?" I said.

"I know you are sometimes sad," he said, "because you do not smile. I know you are sometimes lonely because you do not laugh."

We were both silent for a moment and I marveled at

how quickly he understood. And how natural it seemed that he should be sitting at my table drinking coffee.

He pushed back his cup and rose from the table and walked to the door. I followed him there and he turned and paused with his hand on the knob. He bent a little and kissed me. A quick impulsive kiss that brushed my lips with the grace of the spring wind.

I stepped back shocked.

"You had no right!" I said. "You should not have done that."

"I wanted to kiss you," he said and smiled wickedly. "I do what I want."

Then he was walking swiftly with long strong strides through the rain. My heart flew after him.

THAT NIGHT the family gathered again. All the rosy-cheeked wives and the multitude of children. I worked with a jubilation I found hard to conceal. I even sang a little to myself and several times noticed one of my brothers watching me strangely.

At the end of the meal the children scrambled from the table to resume playing in another room. The wives picked up the plates and carried them to the kitchen. Niko, the youngest of my brothers, caught my arm.

"What makes you sparkle tonight?" he said. "I have never seen you like this before." He gestured at Papa. "What has happened to this girl?"

I tried to shake off his hand but he laughed and held me tight. All of them watched me and I felt my cheeks flaming.

"She is blushing," Marko cried. "Blushing like a school-girl."

"Let me go," I said to Niko, "or I will bring this plate of bones across your head."

"She is in love!" Kostas roared. "The girl's in love!"

A reverent quiet descended upon the room. The wives came from the kitchen to stand in the doorway with their eyes open to great bursting cups. Niko let me go slowly. All of them watched me in some kind of awe.

"Rhodanthe," Papa said and there was a great joy stirring in his voice. "Is this true?"

My heart went out to him. He was growing old and loved me so much. I looked at each of my brothers and felt a great wave of affection for them. I could even forgive their smug wives, secure in marriage to good men, who listened in the doorway.

"Yes," I said. "Yes."

"Thunder and lightning!" Kostas roared. He beat with his big fist upon the table. The dishes rattled and jumped.

"Hurrah!" Niko cried.

"I'll be damned!" Marko shouted.

Everybody looked at Papa. He silently made his cross and looked as if he were about to cry.

"God be praised," he said and his voice trembled. "I knew you must come to your senses. I have brought you some good men. Which one of them have you reconsidered?"

"Five bucks to a buck it's Makris!" Niko shouted.

"That grease pot?" Kostas cried. "She wouldn't touch him with a yardstick."

"It must be Gastis!" Marko said. "It has to be Gastis!"

"Silence!" Papa roared. "Silence!"

The room went quiet. No sound except for the shrieking children in the parlor.

"Silence those little monsters!" Papa roared again. One of the wives went quickly to the parlor and a moment later silence fell in every part of the house. She came back and softly closed the door.

"Which one is it?" Papa spoke to me gently.

I stood at the foot of the table and folded my hands. I took a deep breath and for one brief moment closed my eyes and then opened them again.

"It is none of the men you have brought home," I said.

They all looked shocked. A rumbling began around the table. Papa waved his hand fiercely for silence.

"I do not understand," he said slowly. "It is not Gastis or Makris or Sarantis or Gerontis or any of those other good men?"

"No, Papa," I said.

"Who the devil is it then?" Marko said angrily.

A flare of panic seized me but I had gone too far to turn back.

"A young man who passes on his way to work in the morning," I said. "He has dark and curly hair and he whistles in a way I have never heard anyone whistle before."

For a long startled moment no one spoke.

"She has gone nuts!" Kostas cried. He looked around for confirmation.

"Who is this guy?" Marko shouted. "I'll teach him to whistle at my sister!"

"Dirty hoodlum!" Niko spit between his teeth.

Papa beat with his fist upon the table. Everyone became quiet again.

"You are joking?" Papa said and he made an effort to laugh and one of the wives began to laugh with him. Papa stopped laughing and glared at her and she almost choked closing her mouth.

"I am not joking," I said. "He is a young man that I have spoken to a number of times. This morning we had coffee together."

"He had coffee with you this morning?" Marko shouted angrily. "In this house alone with you?"

"We'll have his teeth hot from his mouth!" Kostas cried.

"Dirty hoodlum!" Niko shouted. "Sneaking behind our backs."

"Who is he?" Papa cried. "Who is he?"

"I don't know his name," I said. I knew how that sounded but I flung at them because I was becoming angry too.

Papa exploded for all of them. Shock and anger ripping his face. The wives cowered in the doorway.

"You don't know his name!" Papa thundered. "You don't know his name!"

They all began roaring at once. I bit my lips hard trying to stop the tears that burned to break from my eyes.

"I don't know his name!" I cried angrily. "I don't know his name! I know I love him! I heard him whistling and saw him and everything changed. This morning it rained and I could have cried because I would not see him and then he knocked on the window." They all sat staring at me and I struggled furiously to find words to overwhelm them. "There were other men I might have loved years ago," I said. "Men who were frightened off by your shouts and your fists. But you will not take this man from me. He told me he knew I was sad because I did not smile and that I was lonely because I did not laugh and then he kissed me!" I felt a tremor shake my body and my voice rose fiercely. "I don't know his name! I only know I love him!"

THEY WERE sorry afterwards. Papa came to my room and kissed me and cried a little. Then Marko and Niko and Kostas came and touched my hair gently with their big hands and tried to speak with their eyes. I forgave them because I knew how much they cared for me. And I consented to let Niko wait with me in the morning to see the young man.

But he did not come the next morning. I thought perhaps he knew about Niko and the following day I waited alone. I waited in the yard with the spring wild and tangled about my head and the blossoms breaking on the branches of the trees and the earth flowing and alive.

He did not come. And the spring passed into summer and the leaves grew long and green on the trees and the sunflowers bloomed among the stones and the birds were everywhere. The speckled robins and the gray starlings and the brownish redwings.

After a while I knew Papa and the others thought I had made it all up. That I had grown weary of the procession of sad suitors and made the story up to keep others away.

They do not understand that someday he will come back. On a morning when the green hearts of the lilac bushes tremble awake in the wind. When the first slim green buds break upon the branches of the maples and the catalpas.

He will come striding along with his hands in his pockets and his reckless head flung back and the wild jubilant whistle ringing from his lips. And I will feel once again that the early green buds and the first fragile flowers and the soft new winds have suddenly burst into song.

A HAND
FOR TOMORROW

In the fifteen years since the end of the Second World War many changes had come to Bleecker Street. The Quality Delicatessen, which had once specialized in a fragrant potato salad, had been joined with a lunchroom and a small hand laundry to form a glistening supermarket dominating the street. Banners with great red letters and numbers were splashed across the windows, and shiny shopping carts rolled in and out of the parking lot all day. Farther down the street, the little dusty tailor shop of Max Feldman, who claimed at one time or another to have pressed the pants of every male within a mile radius of Bleecker Street, had been demolished along with a radio repair shop and a candy store to make a bright and gaudy drive-in cleaners operated by his sons.

Of all the stores that had existed on the street before the war, only the small grocery of Kostas Stavrakas remained unchanged except for concessions to the miracles of modern packaging.

Kostas, ignoring the trend to health breads and protein breads and enriched breads, still baked his own loaves as he had baked them for thirty years in the oven in the back room of his store. He carried an assortment of Balkan spices and Greek and Bulgarian cheeses white as the foam on fresh-whipped milk. Although he had accepted the utility of neon lighting and had purchased a small sign to hang in his window, his store stood out at night by appearing almost an island of darkness beside the flaming, garish splendor of the rest of the street.

What little business he did came mostly from the older people who had traded with him for years. As they died or moved away, there was nobody to replace them. In the meantime he did some business in the morning before the supermarket opened and in the evening after it closed.

He did not mind the leisurely pace of his trade. For some years now his legs had been bothering him, and he wore shoes slit along the sides to ease the swelling of his feet. But he could not conceive of existence away from the store in which he had spent thirty years. When his wife was alive, they had planned together for his retirement, but after her death of a stroke, a few years before, this dream had lost relevance. He lived with his married son and wife, who had a two-year-old daughter whom Kostas adored. This family and the store with the warm, familiar scents of spices and cheese and yeasty bread hot from the oven were the boundaries of his life.

THE AFTERNOONS were long and quiet, and shortly after lunch he would be joined each day by his old friend, Max Feldman, the tailor whose shop had been surrendered to the ambitions of his sons and the cornucopia of progress. They would gravely set up the checkerboard within arm's reach of the briny pickles in the barrel.

"Where does the count stand?" Max asked, and puckered

his thin, dry lips and wriggled his crooked ears. "I must be leading by a dozen games this month."

"No more than three," Kostas said. "You have no conception of the difference between addition and multiplication."

Max shrugged that off. "This will be a short, sad game," he said. "Five, maybe six of Feldman's murderous moves and, pfft! you will be gone."

"Your best game is with your mouth," Kostas said. "If hot air counted, you would be champion checker player of the world."

"Play!" Max cried. "Today I have no mercy!"

They made their first moves and settled down to the game, staring intently at the board. They played in a tight silence until the door of the store opened and a little bell jingled. A gray-haired heavy woman entered. Kostas rose to serve her.

"Don't cheat," he said in a soft warning whisper to the tailor. Max looked outraged.

"Good day, Mrs. Lanaras," Kostas said warmly. "How is your fine son, Thanasi?"

"Still growing," Mrs. Lanaras said, "and eating enough for three grown men. How is your family?"

"Excellent, thank you." Kostas smiled. "At two years of age my granddaughter is as beautiful as Aphrodite. Can I help you?"

"A little cheese, I think," Mrs. Lanaras said. "A half-pound of feta and a loaf of bread. Thanasi takes four sandwiches for lunch."

Kostas packed the items, rang up the sale, and Mrs. Lanaras walked briskly out the door.

"Yesterday as I was coming," Max said, "I saw her and that lummox Thanasi carry two bags out from the supermarket. Bags loaded like that only giants should carry. Here she comes to buy a little cheese and a loaf of bread.

Such customers should do you a favor and pass by without stopping."

"She was good to come in for that," Kostas said. "The supermarket has a counter with cheeses from all over the world and varieties of bread. I am grateful she comes in for anything at all."

Max looked for a long, searching moment at Kostas. "Tell me something," he said slowly. "Are you making expenses?"

"Certainly!" Kostas said in a shocked voice. "What kind of businessman do you think I am? Every month a small profit is made here, although I admit not what it used to be."

"What about your son, Nick?" Max asked. "Does he still come sneaking in with a carpenter and an electrician under his jacket?"

"They were in here again last week," Kostas said and smiled. "They took measurements for hours and scribbled a padful of figures. Nicolas is so excited. He wants to do so much. I tell him to wait. When I am dead he can do what he wishes with the store."

Max shook his head somberly. "Believe me, they can't wait," he said. "Don't I know? Twenty-seven years in one location they should let a man walk out, but from my store they shot me like a shell out of a cannon. They came to me one afternoon and said, 'Papa, tomorrow the wreckers will be here.'" His lips curled with contempt. "A drive-in cleaners they wanted. So lazy louts never lift their rumps from the car. A girl they got in a short skirt and naked legs to take the clothing right from the car. Believe me, they can't wait."

"You admit yourself they are making a lot of money," Kostas said.

"Money, money!" Max cried. "Do me a favor and stop

talking about money. A little money a man should make
to live, but with dignity." He flung his arm up and cut
the air violently. "Imagine! A drive-in cleaners with a girl
in a short skirt and naked legs to take the clothing from
your car!"

THE DOOR of the store opened, and the bell jingled again.
Nick Stavrakas came in. He was a tall, thin young man
with a serious twist to his lips and black curly hair and
intense eyes.

"Hi, papa," he said. "Hello, Max."

He stood for a moment balancing on the balls of his
feet. He looked up to the ceiling, and a shadow of annoyance crossed his cheeks. "Papa, that light is still burned
out. I thought you were going to get Leon to fix it?"

"I forgot to tell him yesterday," Kostas said. "I will tell
him for sure today."

"You can hardly see the canned-goods labels on the
center shelf with the light on," Nick said. "With the
light out, the shelf is in total darkness."

"I'll be sure he fixes it today," Kostas said quickly.

Max smiled slyly at the young man. "Tell me, how are
all your friends?" he said. "The carpenters and electricians."

Nick frowned at the old tailor. "If you don't mind,
Max," he said. "I wanted to talk to papa alone for a
minute."

Max sighed and rose slowly from his chair. "I'll take a
walk to the park and watch the pretty nursemaids for a
while," he said. "There is one Bathsheba who is like
a juicy strudel."

"Sit down, Max," Kostas said. "We have no secrets
from you." He looked gently at his son. "You have some
more estimates?"

With a final despairing glance at Max, Nick pulled

a sheaf of papers from his pocket. When he spoke, his voice was vibrant with excitement. "Papa, these estimates are the best yet!" He motioned eagerly with his hand. "This plan would almost triple the area usable and let us stock three times the items we carry."

"How?" Kostas asked.

"By knocking down that wall," Nick said, "opening those partitions in the rear and utilizing all that lost space."

"What about my oven in the back room?" Kostas asked.

Nick shook his head fretfully. "That would have to go," he said. "That takes up space and yields nothing."

Max gave a sharp, pointed laugh and looked intently at the checkerboard. Kostas looked quickly at his friend and tried not to smile.

"Papa," Nick said, and his voice rose a little, "you know that oven is outdated. It costs you forty cents to bake a loaf of bread that you can't sell for more than thirty. In the supermarket, people get their choice of forty kinds of bread."

"Fifty kinds," Max said sagely. "Once I counted them."

"I have been baking bread for families here for thirty years," Kostas said.

"Papa," Nick said excitedly. "That kind of business you can afford to lose. We've got to streamline this store. Do you know that Tony Manteno, the real-estate broker, was telling me this block is a gold mine for business? This block draws a fantastic number of people. We've got to get our share."

"We do a fair business," Kostas said. "We make a fair profit on the items we sell."

"Not one-tenth the business we could if we remodeled," Nick said. "Papa, I've racked my head to plan every step. I tell you we can't lose. We would have our additional investment back in a couple of years."

Kostas did not answer for a moment. "I know there is truth in what you say," he said slowly. "Let me think about it a little more."

"Papa," Nick said in exasperation. "You've been saying that for three years, and you haven't made a move."

Kostas walked from the counter to the window. He stood silently for a moment, looking at the people walking past.

"Thirty years is a long time," he said finally. "Children who stood with their eyes open like big saucers before the jars of three-for-a-penny candy are grown into adults and married, with children of their own. Friends who once came in and sat and smoked and sipped a glass of wine have grown old, and some have died. This store has many memories."

"Papa," Nick said, and a softness entered his voice, "memories are fine, but you can't live today in a dream of the past. You've got to keep up."

"They can't wait," Max said somberly, as if he were speaking to himself. "They can't wait."

Kostas turned back to his son. "All this new business," he said, "will mean additional help. I have always managed this store alone. People who come in expect me to look after them."

"We would need some help," Nick said. "You could begin to take it easy and supervise everything. Sort of keep your eye on the whole operation."

"Tell me," Max asked sharply. "Do you think you might use a girl in a short skirt with naked legs?"

Nick looked at him in irritation. "What does that mean?"

"Nothing," Max said innocently. "I just happen to know where there is one such girl available."

"Nicolas," Kostas said. "We will talk further this evening. We will examine the figures together." He nodded at Max. "This boy has a marvelous head for figures," he said proudly.

"Papa," Nick said, "I know talking about this makes you unhappy, but something has to be done. I've become the laughingstock of the street. Always estimates and figures and plans and nothing more. Think of me."

Kostas looked for a long, silent moment at his son. "I am always thinking of you," he said softly. "Of you and Lucy and Katerina. The three people I care most about in this world."

Nick lowered his head to conceal the flush risen suddenly to his cheeks. "I'm sorry, papa," he said. "I know how much you think of us." He paused for a moment and tasted his defeat and could not resist one final assault. "Look now," he said, and his voice shook under an effort to speak quietly. "I've been in here almost twenty minutes now, and not one customer has entered in that time. Do you call this a business? It's more like a cemetery."

"I am a small grave on the hill," Max said wryly. "Before you leave, water my plot."

Kostas could not help smiling. Nick glared in sudden anger from one to the other. "Laugh!" he said shrilly. "Laugh and sit in this cemetery and play checkers all day. At least admit you aren't really in business. You don't want this place to become a business because it would interrupt your game. You sit in here, and outside the world has changed, and you go on playing checkers and ignoring burned-out lights."

"Nicolas," Kostas said with concern.

"I'm sorry, papa," Nick said. "I'm fed up! I'm your only son and I love you more than anything else in the world, and I swear to God I want what is best for you and Lucy and the baby. I'm full of energy and ambition, and I want to repay you for all the good years and take care of you, and all you can do is sit and worry about playing checkers."

He turned and stumbled once in his haste and then went quickly out the door.

"They can't wait," Max said grimly. "They can't wait."

Kostas returned to his chair and sat down and shook his head in despair. "Maybe we are the selfish ones," he said. "We have forgotten what it is like to be young." He paused and looked around the dimly lighted store, breathing the warm, familiar scents that came from the darkened shelves and the hidden corners. "Maybe the boy is right," he said. "Maybe this place is a cemetery."

Max shook his head violently. "Better a cemetery than a circus!" he cried. "A circus with a girl in a short skirt and naked legs so the lummoxes won't raise their rumps from the car. Big, flashing neon signs and tinsel waving like every day is the Fourth of July."

"They are young," Kostas said sadly. "The world seems to move by quickly if they fall out of step. They cannot bear to be left behind." He shook his head in some stricken wonder. "Where has the time gone?" he said. "It seems like yesterday that we pushed their buggies in the park on Sunday afternoons and wiped their running noses and dreamed of their growing up to be President of the United States." He stared at the board without seeming to see the checkers. "Now my Ethel is gone, and your Sarah is gone. The babies are grown into men who live in a world different from the one we remember. And the time goes by so swiftly."

Max pulled out his handkerchief and blew his nose in a harsh trumpeting of sound. "Move!" he said. "It's your move for a half-hour now. You are maybe planning to move sometime before closing? Do me a favor and move, why don't you?"

They finished their third game late in the afternoon. Max dozed a little in his chair, his bald and bony head nodding slightly. Kostas quietly swept out the store. When Leon, the maintenance man, came in, Kostas had him replace the burned-out bulb. A few customers came in for several small purchases.

As TWILIGHT fell across the street and Kostas turned on the window light, Nick returned. He brought his wife, Lucy, and their daughter, Katerina, sitting upright in her stroller.

Kostas saw them coming and held the door so Nick could push the stroller in. He looked quickly at his son's face to see what vestige of the morning's disturbance remained. Then he forgot everything in his pleasure at seeing his grandchild.

He lifted her squealing from the stroller. He kissed her warm, soft cheeks and raised her high above his head. She shrieked with delight, and he held her close and poked her gently with his nose.

Lucy, a pretty, slender, dark-haired girl, kissed him on the cheek. "We have lamb and green beans for supper tonight, papa," she said gently. "I fixed them especially for you. Nick and I came to watch the store so you can go home and eat while the food is still warm."

Kostas looked at Nick, and for a moment the young man did not meet his father's eyes. Then Nick managed a slight, repentant smile, and Kostas smiled in warm and grateful response.

"Lamb and green beans?" Max said, coming out of the

shadows. "Is there perhaps enough for an old tailor who eats no more than a sick baby?"

"All sick babies should eat as well as you," Kostas said. "They would become well in a hurry."

"Always enough for you, Mr. Feldman," Lucy said. "You go along and keep papa company."

"There is plenty of food," Nick said. "Lucy cooks enough for six men."

"She knows lamb and green beans are my favorite," Kostas said proudly to Max. He patted his daughter-in-law's cheek with tenderness and affection. "I am a lucky man. I have a fine son, and he married a grand girl, and together they produced this incomparable child." He made a face at the baby.

"My sons married monsters," Max said somberly. "Wailing harpies who cook like poisoners. Believe me, every meal at their table freezes my blood."

Nick took the child from his father and returned her to the stroller. He gave her some cellophane-wrapped candy canes to play with. A customer entered, and Kostas started behind the counter. Lucy waved him away. "I'll take care of the store, papa," she said. "You and Mr. Feldman get started now. The lamb will become cold."

NICK WENT into the back room and returned with his father's jacket. He held it for Kostas to put on.

"Papa," Nick said, and he spoke softly so that only his father could hear. "I'm sorry about this morning."

"It was not your fault you became angry," Kostas said quickly. "Max and I should not have laughed."

"No, papa," Nick said, and shook his head in muted despair. "I've been thinking about it all afternoon. I talked to Lucy for two hours. I been fooling myself for a long time, but I got no right to change you or change the store. Anybody who has worked as many years as you have worked this store has got a right to keep it just the way he wants."

"Nicolas," Kostas said. "I am not saying my way is right."

"Let me finish, papa, please," Nick said. "I guess I'm not as smart as I think sometimes, but when I stop and figure it out, a light begins to dawn. I've been bothering you for three years, but you don't have to worry or become upset any more. Starting now, I'm through with estimates and figures. I'm going to leave you alone about the store. That's the way Lucy and I decided."

Kostas looked silently at his son for a long time and then impulsively embraced him. He held him tightly for a moment and then, suddenly self-conscious, stepped away quickly, looking to see if Max or Lucy had noticed. He turned his face slightly and spoke slowly and carefully. "This is my store," he said quietly. "And I have made up my mind what must be done. This place is a disgrace. It was fine for thirty years ago, but it has become a rusty bicycle on a street of fast new cars. Changes must be made."

"Papa," Nick said, and he shook his head in wonder. "What are you saying?"

Kostas did not trust himself to touch the boy again. "I've made up my mind I want to see what you can do for me," he said briskly. "I am not that bad a businessman. I am satisfied you have looked into the matter thoroughly, and I put my faith and trust in you. Don't let me down."

"Papa," Nick said angrily. "You're doing this because of what I said this morning. You're doing this because of me. I won't have it."

"Will you shut up about this morning?" Kostas cried.

"Am I a child that a few words spoken in excitement cause me to change my mind? I am not married to this old store. It has provided me a living and memories, but it has also given me swollen feet and aching legs. Now go and help your wife and let me go home and eat my lamb and green beans, and in the morning call the carpenters and electricians and make plans for the work to get started."

As HE finished speaking, Max came silently to stand at his side. Nick turned on the tailor with enthusiasm. "Did you hear, Max?" he cried. "Papa and I are ready to go! We are going to make this the finest little store on the street! We'll show them all!" He turned fervently to his father. "Just wait! You won't be sorry! I'll make you proud!" He turned and walked quickly toward his wife.

"They can't wait," Max said softly. "And because they are flesh of our flesh, we give in."

Kostas watched Nick talking earnestly to Lucy. He turned on Max. "The trouble with you, Feldman," he said loudly, "you live in the past. You lack vision. Your sons were right to throw you off the premises. You have a brooding face that invites disaster and despair."

He started for the door, and after a moment of outraged silence Max followed. Lucy and Nick called to Kostas and started toward him, but he waved them away. "Later," he said. "The lamb and beans grow cold. Later."

He fled to the street. Max followed him out, and when he caught up, the old tailor laughed dryly.

"Moses Stavrakas," he sneered. "So I lack vision. I live in the past. You rushed out of that store because maybe in another minute you would have been crying. Ha!"

Kostas glared at him and did not speak. He walked with as quick a stride as his swollen feet would allow, and the tailor had to half run to keep up.

"You know what this means?" Max paused for a moment to catch his breath. "The song is familiar. When all the painting and renovating has been finished, the only old antique left sticking out of place is you."

"I know," Kostas said. "I know."

"But do not despair," Max said, and he laughed a dry, ironic laugh. "I will be here to help you. I will teach you to sit in the park and watch the pretty nursemaids and argue politics with the Irishmen who sit like black roosters in the sun. I know the best benches for checkers, the ones shaded beneath the trees. And when the weather turns cold, there is always the public library with newspapers from all the big cities."

"Feldman!" Kostas said wrathfully "Feldman, go to the devil!"

They walked on together without speaking. They passed under the bright, flashing glitter of the signs and the neon night streaked with multicolored lights. As they approached the great, gleaming festival of the supermarket, Max fell a step behind and fiercely brandished his fist at the long window with flaunting banners, and with a violent gathering of his body he spat on the ground before the store.

THE PASSING
OF THE ICE

THAT MORNING, standing before Toby's desk in the dispatch office, Mike felt the moment of his discharge had come. The straw boss sat overflowing his chair with the great rolls of fat around his waist and loins, his heavy fingers leafing through the papers on the desk.

"How you feel today, Mike?" Toby asked.

"I feel fine," Mike said. "I feel like an iceman. How do you feel?"

"You look tired, Mike," Toby said. "A man should not look as tired as you so early in the morning."

"We are all tired," Mike said. "But a heavy man covers his weariness and a skinny man shows it to the bone."

The straw boss sat stiffly at the desk staring intently at the papers, as if he had forgotten anyone was there. His way was to loosen his grip just enough to allow a man to think he might escape, and then clamp his big hand on him tighter. Mike had seen others squirm and sweat before the desk. He showed no fear, because his dread was not of the fat man but of being forced to accept the measure of his days.

"Somebody left ice out." Toby spit the words between his thin lips. "An old hand like you should watch there is no goddam ice left on the trucks overnight."

"I'll watch," Mike said.

Outside the office the loaded trucks stood idling with the blocks wedged beneath the wheels. The voices of the drivers and helpers carried in a chorus of curses and laughter. J. C. would have his truck gassed and loaded with the cakes of four-hundred-pounders stacked to the tailgate.

"Why don't you give up?" Toby said, and his voice was a harsh and ugly whisper. "You can't move around on the cars like you used to. It won't be long anyway."

Mike felt a violence deep in his belly, the fury of a temper that had plagued his younger days. He waited until the hard knot eased, and tried to speak quietly.

"I get around," he said. "I work twice as hard because I know you don't want to lose me."

"Get out." Toby's eyes were bright in anger. "Get out, old man, and do your work."

Mike left the office. Outside he stood for a moment in the spring morning with the smell of the earth fresh and cool, and found himself trembling. He walked across the roadway to where J. C. waited in the cab of the truck, feeling that Toby had risen from his desk and was watching at the window.

"Roll your truck, Mike," Sargent cried from behind the wheel. "We late now."

On the running board of the next truck, tall and lean-flanked Noodles swung an arm toward the sky.

"O sun," Noodles sang. "You have displayed your backside long enough. Winter has been fierce and the icemen are weary. O sun, grow strong and warm poor old Noodles."

From the tailgate of Noodles' truck, his helper Gomez waved a greeting to Mike.

"This is the season," Gomez said, turning his face to the sky, "the time I would like to own a small farm and work in the fields."

"You, a farmer?" Noodles said. "Gomez, you couldn't grow foam on a glass of beer."

"You making noise with your mouth," Gomez said. "My father was a farmer. I would have been a good farmer."

"Sure you would have," Mike said. "Lay off quail hunting every night with Noodles, and save your money. Get back to the farm."

When Mike reached his truck, J. C. kicked out the blocks that wedged the wheels and swung into the cab beside him.

"Let 'em roll!" Mike shouted savagely. "C'mon, you dead-rumped coal hikers that call yourselves icemen. Roll them loads!"

Noodles waved and hollered something that was lost in the roar of the motors.

A few moments later, driving with the windows open and the air cool against his cheeks, Mike's trembling had eased. J. C. rode in silent fury beside him.

"The bastard was on you again," J. C. said. "The bastard was riding your back again." His black cheeks corded, and each curse came bitten from his mouth.

"What you talking about?" Mike said. "He poured me a cup of coffee and shared his chocolate doughnut with me. You got that big and friendly man all wrong."

They looked at each and smiled. J. C. laughed. Mike felt the old pleasure returning, the rocking feel of the wheel in his hands, the pull of the loaded trailer, and a good friend beside him.

"You can smell the spring," Mike said. "In a few more weeks the summer, and then another year almost gone."

"To hell with the season," J. C. said. "Icemen freeze in winter and roast in summer. You know the ice don't care what time of year."

"Amen," Mike said.

MIKE KNEW the ice. He had worked with the pick and tongs for almost forty years. Sometimes in the summer, with the dry railroad cars waiting to be iced, and in his rushing back to the hill to reload, he forgot for a little while that the icing was not the way it had been. Bungo was dead, and the great Orchowski no longer roared his wild songs from the top of the cars. Each year brought more icing machines, and the old icemen were gone. Now in the beginning of summer the young wandering Negroes and the Irish gandy dancers came to work on the trucks. They were strong without skill and lifted to show off their strength. Foolish young men who tried to lift the three- and four-hundred-pound blocks with their backs or with their arms. Mike tried to teach them how to lift by using their legs and how to hook the tongs just the right distance from the score marks. But he worked beside them uneasily, aware how a man could be maimed or crushed by the carelessness of others.

There were a few good men among them. J. C., the young Negro on his truck, had some of the strength and spirit of the old icemen. Noodles knew how to handle his Hilift. The dark and bitter Sargent could cut and throw the way Chino once had. But they were just a few among the sportive young men who came for the summer pay and took no pride in their work and left wearily in the autumn.

Mike had been the smallest of the giants, and now he was alone. But time and the ice had not left him untouched. Each year the burden of his back and legs began earlier in the day, until by the middle of the afternoon his muscles were knotted and each movement of icing was scored with pain. More and more often he was seized with a strange despair that he could not go on icing any longer.

He could not do much of anything else. He could eat and drink and sleep and in season go to see a ball game. He could lie in the darkness next to Zeba and sometimes still feel the wild and sudden tenderness that briefly let his weariness drop aside. Afterward he could not help but laugh, remembering himself as a bantam rooster and the women as the hens. Of all the women he had known and loved, only Zeba remained. She had never been very pretty, and she was no longer young. Little pouches of flesh had gathered beneath her chin, and in the morning he noticed how the strap of her slip was held by a pin, or how the seam of her stocking might run all around her leg. But in the evening there was hot food on the table. When he brought J. C. home, she baked them spareribs and went down to the corner and brought them back cold beer. She was kind to his friend, and for this he was grateful. When it was time to go to bed, Zeba rubbed Mike's back and legs with ointment, her big warm hands bringing a temporary comfort to his body. Afterward they lay side by side, and she spoke of the years they had spent together. She talked low and soft in the dark room, and knowing his weariness, she did not ask a question or expect him to say a word. Sometimes she laughed at something she remembered, secretively, yet always including him. He would feel himself easing into the darkness and her voice fading and the last low stirrings of her laughter.

"How come I let you be my driver?" J. C. bared his teeth

in a broad grin. "You too skinny to be a good driver for a big boy like me."

"Fat ass don't make a good iceman," Mike said.

J. C. laughed and struck his big fist against his chest.

"Never been an ice crew like us," he said. "Someday we going to ice together in hell. Damn devil going to say, 'J. C., where that skinny driver you come down with? Oh, there he is hiding in the cab. All right, now you both here, let the number-one ice crew start to work and cool off hell.' "

"You crazy." Mike smiled. "I taught you all I know, and now you wear your pants too high. Between tall pockets and big feet you got a head like a sponge."

"I'm an iceman," J. C. said. "All icemen got a sponge for a head. It goes with the job."

"Amen," Mike said.

When they reached their first stop, at the Harley Depot, the yardmaster located their cars on the spur. Mike pulled the truck alongside the first car to be iced, and carrying picks and tongs, he and J. C. swung up on the back of the truck.

The elevator rose slowly to the height of the car. They began to work, cutting the blocks into chunks to fit the bunkers. Swiftly they fell into the rhythm, and the ice flew. To save their wind they did not speak, but J. C. hummed a broken snatch of melody. Their picks rose and fell, and the ice split into chunks for the tongs to grab and throw. They moved quickly and surely on the narrow runway. They closed the lids and lifted the plugs with a steady pull. As fast as they finished a car they moved on to the next.

A little past noon they stopped for lunch at Chino's small bar on Laramie Street. They ordered beef sandwiches garnished with pickle and onion, and steins of lager beer.

Sitting in a rear booth of the darkened room, Mike was grateful for the chance to rest among the warm shadows.

Chino, bent with arthritis but still taller than most men, came to sit in the booth with them. He had been one of the icemen with Mike in the days of Bungo and Orchowski. When his joints became inflamed and his body twisted, he bought an interest in the small bar. He kept it shadowed, as if ashamed to be seen by the men who still worked the trucks.

"How's business, Chino?" Mike asked.

"Ain't doing nothing," the old iceman said gloomily. "We get a little movement at lunch, and the rest of the day is like a graveyard. See." He motioned with his stiff and swollen fingers around the room.

"Sure," J. C. said. "You stop watering your beer and stop making sandwiches so skinny, you get some more business."

"You just a punk," Chino said. "You don't know like Mike and me know. The ice is passing. There ain't no more trade from the locations. In a few more years the machines will do all the icing and the last icemen will be working in the goddam coalyards."

Mike shut his eyes, and for a moment the years fell away and he worked with Bungo and Orchowski, and Chino was a tall young giant, wilder than all the rest.

"You remember?" Chino said. "Mike, you remember how it used to be?"

"I remember," Mike said.

Chino twisted his head around like a frightened bird suddenly trying to take flight. He raised his hand from the table and held it for a moment poised in the air and then slowly lowered it again to the scarred surface of the wood.

"It ain't no use thinking about how it used to be,"

Chino said. "I think and think but it ain't no use. Things are just the way they are and nothing can change them. The old ice days are gone, and they ain't never going to come back."

J. C. finished the last of the beer in the stein and wiped his mouth with the back of his hand. "You make it sound like we all dead now," he said.

"You just a punk," Chino said. "You don't remember the ice trucks lined up for blocks. Tarpans and Shaws and the crews from Proviso. A few years back, even after I was off the Hilifts, they would fill this place for lunch. But not one of them a damn iceman like we was in the old days. Ain't that right, Mike?"

Mike stood up to leave, suddenly not wanting to listen to Chino any longer.

"You still talk just as much," Mike said. "By God, Chino, you talk as much now as before."

"I got a right," Chino said. "Business is bad and my back hurts and all I got to do is sit and remember."

"Stuff it," J. C. said. "Trouble with you is you see the whole world hung up. You ain't the only man pushing to see daylight."

"Listen, Chino," Mike said. "Tomorrow make the beef a little leaner. Today was too much fat." He put his hand briefly on the old man's shoulder and felt the block of strength beneath the swollen joints.

Outside, the sunlight hurt their eyes, and for a moment they stood squinting while the shavings of ice melting on the truck dripped into puddles in the gutter.

"He's right about one thing," J. C. said. "You the only iceman left. Rest of us don't count for crap."

"Chino and me make noise with our mouths"—Mike shook his head and spoke gruffly—"because we can't shake our rumps the way we used to."

He climbed into the cab of the truck. J. C. walked to the other side and swung in beside him.

"He's right anyway," J. C. said. "I know the old man is right because you the only hump at the hill don't scare when Toby talks. Rest of us call him bastard but inside we sweat. Maybe it's how you think about the ice. Not like the rest of us, just a job. I see you close and I know."

Mike turned the key, and the motor kicked over with a roar. Then he reached over and brought his bunched fist down hard on J. C.'s leg above the knee. The helper bellowed with a cry of pain that almost drowned the noise of the motor.

"You're right," Mike said. "No one any damn good but me."

J. C. rubbed his leg and began to laugh.

"Daddy," he said. "When I grow up, daddy, can I be an iceman like you?"

They laughed together, and Mike pulled the truck from the curb and started back to the hill to reload.

By the time they got to the big ice storage house at the top of the hill, the rest at lunch had worn off and Mike was aware again of the burden of his body. He backed the truck to the edge of the platform. He waited with his tongs at the ramp while J. C. opened the heavy door and entered the icehouse. In a moment the helper backed out swiftly dragging the first four-hundred-pound block, his powerful back and big-muscled arms handling the ice easily.

Mike watched him and marveled at his strength and realized that even in his prime years he had perhaps not been as strong as J. C. Yet he still could have beaten him at work, because cutting and throwing the ice were like something he had been born to do, the main reason he had been put on earth. Now, like Chino said, it was too late. No good to hide in a dark bar and remember the way it used to be in sunlight. No good to hang with the ice and fall under weariness and age.

"Sometimes," Mike said, and there was a fierce edge to his voice, "I want to drag out that ice and cut it down and throw it as far as I can, throw it to hell and gone. I want to empty the big house once of every last block and scatter every last damn chunk over the hill. Make the fat man sit up. Make everyone understand that after forty years an iceman don't just lay down his pick and tongs with a goddam whimper."

J. C. paused and watched him silently for a long moment and then finally flashed his big white teeth.

"You too little to empty the big house," he said. "A little chewed-up runt like you can't do it alone. You need J. C. help to cut down the big house."

"Shove it," Mike hooted. "The only edge you got is a fat head and feet six sizes bigger than you need."

Together they put on the last blocks to make a full load. They climbed back into the cab, and Mike started the truck down the hill. Another truck passed them going up the hill to reload, and Noodles and Gomez waved from the cab.

In front of the dispatch office, Toby stood by the gas pumps waiting for them.

"Hot dog," J. C. said. "Run over the bastard!"

Mike stopped and braked beside the pumps and kept the motor idling. Toby looked up at him unsmiling, and as he stood there without the partial cover of his desk, the great rolls of fat hung upon his frame and made him appear rooted, like some shapeless and heavy-footed animal, to the earth. In that moment Mike was aware how unlike the icemen the fat man was. Where they were lean and quick, he was leaden and slow. Where they tried to sing in their work, he was angry with envy and reminded them it was a burden.

"You took a long time loading," Toby said.

J. C. shifted restlessly beside him, and Mike did not say a word but marveled suddenly how clearly he saw the place of the fat man in the passing of the ice.

"When you come back in," Toby said, "put any ice left into the big house. Don't let any ice sit overnight on the damn truck."

"OK," Mike said, and for a moment he pitied the fat man and his load.

That night in the darkness of their rooms Zeba moved closer to him in the bed, and her body assaulted the pain that rioted through his bones. He felt the pressure of her full breasts against his arm, and he twisted in the bed, curling closer to her warmth.

"Sleep," she said, and her voice was soft and husky in the darkness. "Sleep, my old rooster, sleep."

He touched her, but there was no desire in his hands and no wish for her to respond. He wanted only to rest, to banish weariness and pain.

When he fell asleep, in a restless dream the first days of the ice returned. He saw again the great heaving horses pulling the dray, hauling the ice with block and tackle. He worked swiftly beside the wild young men and cut and threw, and then he stood alone. There was only the mournful face of Chino and in a mist the lost faces of the giants and over them all the cloud of Toby, soft and angry, waiting for him to fall and for the mountains of ice to crumble.

He moaned in his sleep and felt Zeba's fingers and dimly heard her comforting voice. He moved gratefully against her body and slipped again into fitful sleep.

IN THE beginning of September, the pain which had

cramped his body through the summer eased up. He was not sure whether he felt less weary because of the shorter hours on the truck or the first clear, cool days. In the early twilight, driving back from icing at one of the depots, he sang loudly, and J. C. joined in, and the two of them bellowed over the roaring of the old motor. Later, as they unloaded the few remaining blocks into the big house, a great round and orange moon hung in the sky above the hill.

September was the time of year the drivers and helpers lingered in the locker room after punching out. A few more weeks would see most of them gone, so they talked of the journeys they would make, following the sun. They would recall the rumble of the freights and the small dark towns that swept by in the night and, finally, the great sweet orchards with the ripe fruit like little pieces of sunlight. They talked confidently of returning in the spring, and at those times Mike tried to convince himself that perhaps he and Chino were wrong. The winter would be quiet as it had always been, but in the spring the Hilifts would rock down the hill again. The dry cars with empty bunkers would stand in long trains. The young Negroes would come up from the South, and the husky gandy dancers would tumble in off the freights, and among them would be another Bungo or another Chino, and they would bring the mighty ice days back. Even as he told himself that story, he did not really believe it might be true.

There was a day near the end of September. His pain returned fiercely late in the afternoon as they iced dry potato cars at Dart Street. He stood for a moment uneasy and surprised. It had been weeks since he had felt it quite so sharply.

A little later, uncomfortable in his chest and stomach,

he had to catch his breath, and on a car runway he let go his tongs and straightened up quickly, feeling a cramp knotting in his chest. The ice seemed to become heavier through the afternoon, and by the time they finished their last car and were on their way in, empty, his arms and back felt stiff and raw. When he pulled up the hill and parked, Noodles and Gomez had just unloaded the few blocks of ice left on their truck into the big house, and the four of them walked together down the hill.

The locker room was thick with smoke and laughter and the jubilation of men leaving to eat and meet their women. Mike sat on a bench in the corner beside a paned window and rested his head against the wall. He wanted to wash and change to the clean shirt hanging in his locker, but suddenly he was far too tired for the effort that required. J. C. came over and shook his shoulder gently.

"C'mon, daddy," J. C. said. "Your lady is baking spare-ribs and I'm invited. You feel better after some of them ribs."

Noodles turned from his locker and laughed.

"Couple of pigeons picking for ribs," he said. "Old Noodles going picking for something else with more meat on it than them ribs." He winked broadly and flexed his muscles. "I seen a gal today," he said. "She come out of no place while we was icing and just stand and watch. Pretty gal with big eyes and hair like golden corn."

"Sheik," Gomez said. "Oh, sheik."

"I told her, honey," Noodles said, "honey, you need an iceman?"

"She was shaken with your hot charm," J. C. said. "I bet she took one look at you and fell right down under the wheels of your truck." He laughed down at Mike, who tried to smile against the stiffness in his cheeks and around his mouth.

"She told me—" Noodles said slowly. "She told me she got an electric icebox."

"Sheik," Gomez said, "tell them what you told her then."

"I told her"—Noodles grinned and slapped his leg—"I told that gal wasn't nothing better than hand icing by an iceman who knew his stuff."

"That's what he told her." Gomez shook his head and chuckled.

The room seemed unreal to Mike, the stiffness spreading to his arms and a slow pounding beginning in his head. Through the grimy glass of the window he could see the shadowed rows of frame houses further down the hill with their kitchens lit for supper. And far over the edge of the city the sun had left a strange red glint in the twilight.

"I could tell that gal was crazy about me," Noodles said. "She probably still there waiting for me."

"I had a gal crazy about me once," Sargent said. "Waited for me every night when I got off work. I borrowed two dollars, and we chased down a preacher. Now we got six kids waiting for me every night when I get off work."

Mike wanted to sleep. He felt suddenly that it would be comforting to be able to lay his head down on the bench and close his eyes and have J. C. and the young icemen close by.

"You all right?" J. C. said. "Daddy, you with me?"

The faces of the men around the room blurred, and in quick panic Mike struggled and recalled them and then lost them again. In sweeping darkness and without moving he seemed to be stretching for something just out of reach. A terrible heat suddenly blazed in his chest, and he wanted to cry out, but the wonder of what was happening kept him silent. He was torn by fear and a strange joy. In the moment of deciding which was stronger, the heat burst within him.

The voices of the men fell away and there was silence in the room. J. C. stood beside the bench, and Noodles came to his side.

"He's sleeping," Noodles said. "He just fell down asleep."

The others moved and gathered uncertainly around the bench.

"He's dead," Sargent said quietly. "I seen them in the army. I know the look. He's a dead man."

"You talk crazy!" Noodles snapped at him. "Old Mike just sleeping!"

"Goddam!" Sargent said savagely. "I know a dead man when I see one. Was you in the army and seen the dead piled up like me, you know too."

"Someone call a doctor," Gomez said in a shocked voice. "Someone better go for a doctor."

"He's dead." Sargent shook his head. "Doctor don't do no good for a dead man."

"Jesus Christ," Noodles said, and made a quick sign of the cross. "Jesus Christ."

For the first time J. C. moved and bent slightly to peer closely at Mike and straightened up and looked around at the circle of men with a stunned and terrible grief on his face.

"He was tired and just died," J. C. said. "He been an iceman a long time, and he got tired and he died."

The silence spread again, and no one moved. One of the men cleared his throat, and another shifted restlessly from one foot to the other.

"Phone the fat man," Sargent said. "Tell him to turn off that TV. Tell him an iceman died."

J. C. reached down and put his arms under Mike's back and legs and lifted his body. He held him easily against his chest. He left the locker room, and no one made a move to follow.

He carried the body to the top of the hill. Once or twice he stopped and for a moment stood unmoving beneath the dark sky pinned with a crescent moon. He started walking again toward the row of parked trucks, and bracing the body against his knees, he opened the cab of Mike's truck and slid him in upon the seat. He fumbled on the floor and found Mike's pick and tongs.

He crossed the hill and climbed the ladder to the big house's platform. He opened the heavy door and in the pale light of the moon saw the blocks of ice in glistening rows waiting to be loaded on the trucks in the morning.

He hooked his tongs on a block in the nearest row and dragged it swiftly through the door to the edge of the platform. He swung his pick and split the scored block. The chunks fell apart, and he switched back to tongs and caught up the chunks one after the other, and swinging them between his legs, flung the ice out into the darkness. When he had finished one block he went in and dragged out another and cut it down and again scattered the ice across the earth. He worked faster and faster, and shattered shavings of ice stung his cheeks. He kept dragging out the blocks and cutting them down and heaving the ice into the darkness. His breathing became hoarse and tight in his chest, and he cut desperately and threw more savagely. He dragged out block after block, throwing farther and farther, the chunks cracking against other chunks that littered the ground.

When the big house was empty, he stood for a moment on the platform, his lungs heaving for air, and then with a great and final fling he hurled the pick and tongs far out into the night.

He climbed down the ladder and walked through the field of broken ice back to the truck. In the cab he moved Mike's head gently to rest against his shoulder. He turned the key, and the motor roared like an animal coming awake. He wheeled the truck out of line and started down the hill to take Mike home.